VITAL CONNECTIONS

VITAL CONNECTIONS

A tragic accident.
A traumatic brain injury. A lengthy coma.
When a thirty-three-year-old father is left with the brain function of a
child, what will it take to turn him back into a man and a dad?

Michael J. Klassen and Karen Linamen

Klassen, Michael J.
    Vital connections / Michael J. Klassen and Karen
Scalf Linamen.
    p. cm.
    Includes bibliographical references.
    LCCN 2012947479
    ISBN 978-1-4675-4114-5

    1. Keller, John, 1977---Health. 2. Brain damage--
Patients--United States--Biography. 3. Brain damage--
Patients--Rehabilitation--United States. 4. Executives
--United States--Biography. 5. Neuroplasticity.
I. Linamen, Karen Scalf, 1960- II. Title.

RC387.5.K53 2012   617.4'81044'092
                        QBI12-600186

Contents

Foreword
Brain Injury Just Got Personal

At LearningRx, our focus for years had been helping kids with learning problems improve memory, attention, and thinking skills. To be honest, we had never explored what our one-on-one brain training procedures could do for traumatic brain injuries (TBIs).

Then, in 2007, our center in Colorado Springs had the opportunity to work with a soldier who, while on deployment, suffered multiple TBIs from blasts from roadside bombs, also known as IEDs. This was the first time we had worked with someone with a TBI. The soldier, once an avid reader, had lost his ability to read, remember, and focus. We didn't know how much our brain training procedures could help him, but we were willing to find out.

The results were astounding. As Vice President of Research and Development at LearningRx, I can tell you that even *we* were surprised. This young man's improvements were absolutely life changing.

Over the next two years we began seeing a growing number of clients with traumatic brain injuries. Many of these clients were soldiers; others had been injured as a result of car accidents, school sports, mountain biking and more. We continued to be amazed as we saw *every single client regain some or all of the brain skills that had been lost due to the injury.*

In 2010, we were able to track the impact of one-on-one brain training on a larger scale, when the Washington State Veterans Department asked us to partner with them in a pilot program for soldiers with TBIs. We provided brain training for fifteen Fort Lewis soldiers who were struggling significantly as a result of traumatic brain injuries. At the graduation ceremony for those who had participated in the program, I listened as soldier after soldier explained how LearningRx brain training had literally changed his or her life. Most had been able save their military careers; many had been promoted to even higher positions.*

We began compiling statistics on soldiers with TBIs who had completed our brain training program. In addition to the fifteen Fort Lewis soldiers, by then we had worked with over forty soldiers in our Colorado Springs Brain Training Center. Again, the results were astonishing.**

As were the stories. I remember one soldier whose exposure to multiple IED explosions resulted in the loss of an eye as well as a TBI. His brain injury had impacted his ability to reason, plan, think quickly and multitask. He felt distracted and frustrated. Before brain training, he assumed he would live the rest of his life on disability. After LearningRx brain training, his improvements were so dramatic that he decided to go back to college and get a degree in industrial automation. Three years later, he still stays in touch with his LearningRx brain trainer and is doing great in college; in fact, this past semester he got all A's!

Professionally, I can't tell you how rewarding all of this has been.

And then it got personal.

In early 2011, my dad sustained a brain injury following an infection that landed him in the hospital for a week. When he was finally released to come home, he was far from his normal self. My dad had always been the smartest and sharpest person I knew; suddenly he was struggling with executive functioning skills, processing speed, and long- and short-term memory. A normal conversation with him became very difficult, and his ability to remember anything for even a few minutes was sketchy at best. My dad had been a brilliant researcher and entrepreneur. Now everything he'd been working on before his illness was put on hold.

About that time, after watching a video about John Keller's TBI and remarkable recovery, I realized that brain injury caused by an infection is not all that different from brain injury caused by a bomb or motorcycle accident. Immediately I felt a surge of hope! My family had already been making plans for Dad to work with a LearningRx brain trainer, and after seeing John's video, we didn't wait another day! We got him started immediately.

Today, because of one-on-one brain training, my dad is nearly back to his old self. The wheels in his head are spinning almost as fast as they did before his illness. I can't imagine the pain of having to live with any other outcome.

By the way, my dad happens to be Dr. Ken Gibson, the creator and founder of LearningRx.

Forty years ago, intrigued with the idea of making kids smarter, my father began researching the latest and greatest developments in brain science, then applying what he discovered to helping kids learn better. Before long, his innovative concept of one-on-one brain training had attracted the attention of educators, doctors and researchers across the nation. Little did he know that his cutting-edge techniques would one day change the lives of tens of thousands of children and adults around the world, plus help him regain his own brain skills lost to illness!

If you know someone who is struggling in school, work or just life in general, I want to assure you that there's hope. I can tell you professionally—and now personally as well—that with the right training, the brain can be changed at any age, and mental performance improved in every area of life.

I trust that you'll find John Keller's story a source of inspiration and hope. I know I did.

Tanya Mitchell
Vice President of Research and Development
LearningRx

*To see the statistics on this study, see appendix C

**To see the statistics on this study, see appendix D

Prologue

by John Keller

This is my story and I slept through most of it.

On a beautiful Sunday afternoon in McAllen, Texas, in February of 2008, my life changed forever. And it happened in a fraction of a second. While I was riding my motorcycle, a car pulled out of a parking lot and T-boned me so hard I was practically knocked into a new zip code!

I woke up eleven months later and 350 miles away in a rehab center in Houston, Texas. During my "sleep," I didn't go to heaven or hell. I just blacked out. When I woke up, the first thing I noticed was that I was wearing diapers. My response was just as surreal. I remember looking down and thinking calmly, *It'll probably be hard to pull my jeans up over those diapers.* Beyond that, I knew nothing. I had no idea where I was. I certainly didn't know I'd been in three different hospitals and a nursing home. I didn't know about the traumatic brain injury or the fourteen surgeries, or that I hadn't walked, talked or eaten for almost a year.

The day I walked out the front doors of the hospital—346 days after my accident—even the doctors and nursing staff were saying it was a miracle.

But we soon discovered that my road to recovery was just beginning. More than two years after the accident, my body was healed but my brain was still broken. Of course, just the fact that I was alive was a huge deal, but I needed more. I needed my brain back. I needed my life back. I didn't want to live the rest of my life being a miracle—I wanted to live a normal life. I wanted to be a man again.

As my dad has said, "After someone with a traumatic brain injury comes home, what then? How do you get them back where they can function, have a job, do their thing?"

This is the story of how some folks saved my life and other folks woke up my brain. But it took the folks at LearningRx—a one-on-one brain training company—to turn me from a miracle back into a man.

Traumatic brain injuries and other brain-related challenges are not hopeless. You may not have a brain injury, but you might be facing a different obstacle that's complicating your life. Maybe it's an attention disorder (ADD or ADHD), dyslexia, or a learning disability. Maybe you've had a stroke, or your child has autism. Or maybe you're upset that your memory isn't what it used to be, or that your thoughts are getting fuzzier as you age. I'm living proof that you really can rewire and change your brain. And if there's hope and help for a brain that was as messed up as mine was, I'm guessing there's hope and help for you, too.

Sometimes things happen without warning, in the blink of an eye, in a fraction of a second. But that doesn't mean there's not a plan for your life, or that God hasn't been preparing the right people with the right solutions, getting them ready to intervene just when you need it most. Even if it's at the eleventh hour. Even if it's an answer you never would have imagined in a million years.

And that's what this book is all about.

1

The Appointment

"The Kellers are here," Erin said, poking her head into the doorway of the office.

Sitting at her desk, Gina Cruz acknowledged her assistant with a nod before briefly turning back to the file lying open in front of her. The top sheet showed a colorful graph, the results of the brain skills tests John had taken the week before.

John Keller, age thirty-five, had a story that was both tragic and miraculous. It involved a horrendous accident, an extended coma, a long rehabilitation, and a recovery so dramatic someone could make a movie about it. But more than two years after the accident, John still wasn't 100 percent. Not even 50 percent. Not even close. John's family had come to Gina looking for good news but Gina knew—after seeing John's test results—they were in for the disappointment of their lives.

John's low scores had even surprised Gina. In the years Gina had owned the San Antonio LearningRx Brain Training Center, she'd helped hundreds of clients find solutions for the challenges in their lives caused by autism, ADHD, learning struggles, dyslexia, memory problems— even Alzheimer's and traumatic brain injuries.

But she'd never seen a case as bad as John's.

Gina scooped up the file and stood to her feet, her chair scraping backward on the floor. She knew she could offer hope to the family waiting outside her office. But first she had to deliver some truly devastating news.

In the reception area, a vase of handpicked bluebonnets at the front desk welcomed clients and guests with a burst of blue, a requisite hallmark of springtime in Texas. In a corner of the room arranged with a loveseat and several chairs, two women and a man sat patiently.

After spending eleven months waiting for John to wake up after his accident, John's parents, James and Jan, and his sister Jennifer certainly knew how to bide their time. And today, tired from the four-hour drive to San Antonio from their home in McAllen, Texas, the family was not only patient but uncharacteristically quiet.

The thirtysomething-year-old man waiting with them, however, was anything but quiet! Wearing a collared shirt, jeans and loafers, John emanated energy and words.

> Could they really strengthen and even reroute John's neural pathways, giving him back some or all of the brain function the accident had taken from him?

"Hey Dad! Do you think the Cowboys are going to draft a quarterback to replace Tony Romo? I hope not because Tony's the man! Someday, Dalton's going to play quarterback for the Cowboys and Caden's going to be his wide receiver. And I'm going to be their proud daddy cheering them on from the stands. No, I want to stand on the sideline. Jennifer, do you remember that time when we were playing Sharyland High School and Steve Christian threw me that lob and I dunked it right over my guy? That's kind of what it's going to be like with Dalton and Caden. Wait a minute! Where's my cell phone? Has anyone seen my cell phone?"

"It's on the coffee table next to you," Jennifer answered. The open magazine on her lap suggested that she was reading, but Jennifer couldn't have told you the topic of an article in that magazine if her life depended on it. Her mind was a million miles away as she thought about various therapies they'd tried since John was released from rehab. They'd seen small changes here and there, but nothing had been able to deliver the life changing improvements the family was desperate to see.

But Jennifer nursed a quiet hope. A friend's daughter had experienced huge gains in mental performance after working with a personal brain training coach from LearningRx. That fifth-grader's story was the reason the Keller family had driven to San Antonio today. Could LearningRx really do what they claimed? Could working with one of their personal trainers strengthen and even reroute John's neural pathways, giving him back some or even all of the brain function a tragic accident had taken from him?

John continued chattering in a loud voice. The accident had robbed him of the social filters we develop as we mature. Because of that, John said anything and everything that popped into his mind. His memory had been damaged also, leaving him terrified of forgetting things he wanted to say—another reason he talked fast and loud, interrupting anyone else who tried to speak.

It had been this way for more than a year. John's family had gotten used to the constant white noise.

Despite John's steady stream of phrases, Jennifer stayed lost in her thoughts. John's mother, Jan, responded now and then by murmuring a reassuring "Yes, John," or patting his hand.

His dad, James, was too busy reading to respond much. Flipping through a three-ring notebook he'd picked up from the coffee table in front of him, he was reading story after story of families like theirs who had sat in this very room seeking a better life for themselves or someone they loved. So many families. So many life changing improvements. Could the same thing happen for John?

"Mr. and Mrs. Keller?"

James and Jan stood. Gina reached for the hand of the man she correctly assumed to be John's dad. "You must be James," she said. "It's a pleasure to meet you." Gina had met Jan and Jennifer the week before when John went through the initial testing to assess the condition of his brain skills. After greeting the women, she turned to John with a warm smile.

"Good afternoon, Miss Cruz," John said at the top of his voice. "Are you a Spurs fan? I can't believe how they're dominating the Mavs after losing Game 1. Three wins in a row! Every night a different man is stepping up. I wore a blue shirt today. Do you like it? Blue is one of my favorite colors. My motorcycle had blue flames painted on it. The flames were my favorite part. I really loved that bike…"

John was still talking up a storm as Gina led the family down the hall toward the consultation room.

Halfway there, Jan dropped back a little and watched her husband and son walking side by side. As she did, the sound of John's childish monologue fell away and she remembered watching the two of them together before the accident.

John was tall, nearly six foot five. James, on the other hand, was five eleven on a good day. And their personalities were as dissimilar as their statures: James loved people and process, John loved numbers and results. James saw the big picture, John was a tiger with details. Jan could see them in her husband's office, James relaxed behind his desk, John standing and pacing like a caged cat, as they debated some new money-saving idea of John's.

> If love alone could rescue John from the limitations of his broken brain, he would have been whole a long time ago.

John was vice president of Star Operators, Inc., a family-owned company of thirty-seven convenience stores doing over one hundred million dollars in sales every year. Responsible for contracts, vendors, human resources, and expenses, John had a reputation for being driven, focused and brilliant.

His strategies were usually successful, often cutting-edge, and every now and then extreme—in which case his dad, as company president, exercised his veto power. On those days, James would shake his head, grin and say, "Son, I know you're a genius with the numbers. But we've got these people working for us, and they have families, and we have to think about their welfare. We can't cut things that close."

Jan remembered that, before the accident, her son wasn't much for chit chat. If a staff meeting went too long, he would cut it short by saying, "This meeting is taking too long and it's wasting my time. Time to get back to work." And on days James took the rest of the family to lunch, John usually begged off so he could keep working, keep moving.

They were as different as night and day, those two, but they had tremendous mutual respect. Their differences hadn't kept them from forging a close relationship and running a thriving family business together. And loving each other. That was the most important thing of all. James and John were as close as any father and son she'd ever known.

But if love alone could rescue John from the limitations of his broken brain, her son would have been whole a long time ago.

John was still chattering as Gina led everyone into the consultation room. Vivid purple and green walls made the room feel bright and cozy at the same time. In the center of the room, soft leather couches faced each other over a coffee table made of pine. A couple of chairs completed the seating circle. Jan sat on one of the couches and Jennifer and Gina sat on the other. James claimed one of the chairs.

Instead of gravitating toward a seat, John announced that he had to visit the little boy's room.

"Go back into the hallway, turn right and the bathroom will be the first door on your left," Gina said.

"Turn right, first left. Turn right, first left." John was still repeating the directions to himself as he left the room.

Jan turned promptly to Gina. "If you don't mind, we don't want John to hear anything that might discourage him. If there's any news that isn't good, could you write it down on a piece of paper and hand it to us? That way he won't hear anything that'll get stuck in his head and make it harder for him to get better."

Gina nodded. "Sure, I can do that."

Moments later John returned. "I'm back!" he bellowed before glancing behind him and yelling, "Thanks, Erin!" Stepping over his dad's legs and making his way to the empty spot on the couch next to his mom, he announced loudly to no one in particular, "I got lost, but Erin helped me find my way back here."

As John got settled, Gina thanked everyone for coming, then said,

> "What we do is based on the science of neuroplasticity, which is a fancy name for the brain's ability to change. Our brains are moldable. They're never set in stone. They reorganize, change and grow in response to stimuli and experiences."

"Last week's assessment was really helpful. I've got John's scores right here, but before we go through them, I want to say that every traumatic brain injury is unique. Some people with TBIs struggle with speech or motor skills. Fortunately, neither of these has presented a struggle for John."

John started to interrupt, but his mother stopped him and redirected his attention to Gina.

"John's brain—actually all of our brains—possess seven core skills that make it possible for us to collect and use information," Gina explained. "In other words, these are the skills we use to think and learn. But when there's been a traumatic brain injury, neural connections are damaged, so these skills don't work like they used to. This is why people with TBIs struggle with things like memory, reasoning, communication."

> "So you're saying you can change John's brain?" James asked with interest.

"John's been in all sorts of rehab," Jennifer volunteered.

Gina nodded. "Rehab is great. It helps patients relearn motor skills like walking, and relearn life skills like, say, brushing their teeth. It also helps them adjust their expectations and figure out how to live better within their limitations. But think about this for a moment—"

From where she sat on the couch, Gina leaned forward, her elbows on her knees, and looked in turn at each member of the family. "All that relearning, adjusting and accommodating is great—but it doesn't address or fix the damage to the neural connections that determine how well John's brain works.

"What we do here is completely different. We're not teachers, and our goal isn't adjusting or accommodating. Instead, we focus on all those damaged neural connections. What we do is based on the science of neuroplasticity, which is a fancy name for the brain's ability to change. Our brains are moldable. They're never set in stone. They reorganize, change and grow in response to stimuli and experiences."

"But John's not a kid anymore," Jan said.

"It doesn't matter," Gina replied. "Our brains have this ability our entire lives, from the day we're born until the day we die."

"Focusing on John's damaged neural connections," James repeated. "What exactly does that look like?"

"We'll put John with a personal trainer who will take him through a series of intense mental exercises, an hour a day, five days a week. You know how, when you work with a personal trainer at the gym, you work up a good sweat? Well, working with our trainers creates a mental sweat of sorts. And just like physical exercise stimulates the muscles and body to change, intense mental exercise stimulates the brain to repair, strengthen and even grow new neural connections."

"So you're saying you can change John's brain?" James asked with interest.

"Yes. We can change John's brain." Gina paused and let the family absorb her words. Then she pulled a sheet of paper from the file and laid it on the coffee table. "Here's where John's cognitive skills are right now."

Jan closed her eyes, her mind flashing to her grandsons, John's babies—two-year-old Dalton and four-year-old Caden. Would they ever get their daddy back? A dad who could hold down a job, pack a school lunch, ask them about their day or drive them to a basketball game? A daddy who didn't need help finding the bathroom in his own house?

She suspected she was about to find out.

Opening her eyes, she leaned with her husband and daughter over the graph Gina had laid on the table.

Studying the graph, the most obvious score showed that one of John's strengths was his short-term memory.

"Then why can't he remember where he leaves his phone? Or how to get back from the bathroom?" Jennifer asked.

"Short-term memory, also called working memory, is the ability to remember information while you're in the process of using it," Gina explained. "So, when I told John to take the first right and then the second left to get to the bathroom, he was able to repeat it. But remembering something he heard or did ten minutes ago, or remembering where he left his phone, requires long-term memory, which is a different thing. We'll get to that in a minute.

"Now, this score represents John's visual processing," Gina drew their attention to another dot. "In this, John ranked a little below average, in the forty-second percentile. This score, here, represents auditory processing, which lets John hear sounds in words and is actually the most critical skill for reading. In auditory processing he ranked in the twenty-sixth percentile, which is even lower and explains why he's no longer able to read effectively."

Gina explained that a percentile score indicated where John would stand in a lineup of, say, one hundred people, based on how everyone did on the same test. Being in the twenty-sixth percentile, for example, meant John did better than 25 percent of the group, but not as well as 74 percent.

The graph was essentially offering a snapshot of John's grey matter, a peek into the mysterious workings of his brain. And while the general idea was fascinating, the reality of what John's graph revealed about the condition of his brain was sobering indeed.

"This next score represents John's logic and reasoning, which is the ability to solve

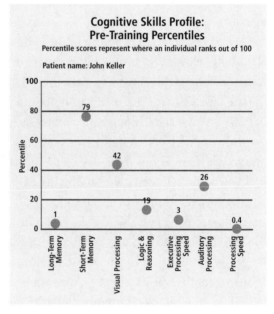

Cognitive Skills Profile: Pre-Training Percentiles

Percentile scores represent where an individual ranks out of 100

Patient name: John Keller

problems. Basically, as children grow up, they're able to understand abstract ideas and solve abstract problems. For example, young children think and talk about themselves. But as they get older, they realize other people have thoughts and feelings too, and they start to share the conversation. John scored very low in logic and reasoning—in the nineteenth percentile—which is one of the reasons he talks only about himself. It's a developmental stage he's reverted to as a result of the injury. But the cognitive skills I'm most concerned about are the last three."

James took a deep breath.

John continued texting friends on his cell phone.

Gina pointed to one of the dots. "This represents John's long-term memory, which is his ability to remember stored information. Remembering where he left his cell phone and how to get back from the bathroom are two examples. Even remembering a thought he just had requires long-term memory. This is another reason John feels compelled to verbalize everything that comes into his head—he knows he's not going to remember it a few minutes from now. John's long-term memory is in the first percentile."

The next two scores were hardly better.

In executive processing—which determines planning, paying attention, solving problems and even regulating thoughts and actions—John scored in the third percentile.

In processing speed, representing how quickly he could handle incoming information, he got the lowest score of all. John's percentile ranking was 0.4—*not even half a percentile!*

In three out of seven critical skills, John's brain was barely functioning. He was hardly showing up on the graph! In that line of one hundred test-takers, John was the last in line. In processing speed, he wasn't even *in* the line.

John's sister and parents were stunned.

"I'm sorry," Gina said kindly. "I know this isn't what you wanted to hear, but the good news is that we can help John. Every day we help people build and rewire neural pathways and significantly change what their brains can do. And John's not the first person with a TBI to go through our program. In one study, sixty U.S. soldiers with brain injuries worked with our trainers, and the improvements were dramatic."

"Gina," Jennifer interrupted, "when my friend's daughter came here, they gave her the age that her brain was functioning at. What age would you give John?

"We don't usually calculate that number for adults, just for kids. For adults we use percentiles, just like we did here with John today."

"But if you *were* to give him an age—" Jan said softly, "especially related to his memory because that's such a huge struggle for him, what would it be?"

John was leaning over the coffee table, trying to stand a pencil on its eraser. He seemed oblivious to the entire conversation. Still, remembering Jan's request not to speak aloud any truly discouraging news, Gina opened her notepad, wrote something down and showed it to Jennifer. Then she tore the page out and handed it to Jan.

Jan stared at the number.

"Let me see it," James asked, taking the paper from his wife. The number on the paper was 4.5.

John was functioning at the level of a child about four and a half years old.

John was playing with his phone again.

James broke the silence. "When do we begin?"

2

Point of Impact

"Erasmo, you'll love it. One ride on my chopper and you'll be hooked."

Pacing the kitchen floor while talking on his cell phone, John continued trying to persuade his cautious friend. "Sunday afternoon... eighty degrees... not a cloud in the sky... what more could you want? Tell you what. I'll pick you up, we'll run by Store 416, and then we'll go see where they're supposed to have that bullfight in McCook tonight."

"No way, man, those things are dangerous. Anyways, your bike is a one-seater. My F-250 gets me where I want to go and Maria doesn't worry about me. Ride your chopper over to my house when you're ready to head to McCook and I'll follow you down in my truck."

"This is your last chance. I just listed it for sale in the *Cycle Trader*. Today's my last ride, then I hang up the keys."

"My loss," Erasmo said, and John could hear the grin in his voice.

John and Erasmo Mendez were friends and colleagues. Together, they ran a chain of Shell® gas station/convenience stores with 350 employees. John was vice president. Erasmo, an area supervisor, dealt with the retail side of the business. Erasmo's wife, Maria, worked in the front office.

Giving up on changing Erasmo's mind, John wrapped up the call, dropped his phone in his pocket and reached for a jar of peanut butter.

April saw the move and frowned. "You're not staying for lunch?" A pretty brunette with petite features, John's wife was sitting at the kitchen table with eight-week-old Dalton and two-year-old Caden.

"Baby, I need to run by 416 and then I'm heading over to McCook." John tossed a bag of bread on the kitchen counter next to the peanut butter. "There's a bullfight tonight and I'm thinking of taking Caden but I want to scout it out first, make sure it would be safe for him. Besides, it's a perfect day for my last ride."

"I wanted you to watch the boys while I went grocery shopping," April said as she frowned again.

"Tell me what you need and I'll pick it up on my way home."

"On your bike? Now that would be entertaining to watch," April replied, smiling despite herself. Then her tone changed, as she wistfully said, "John, I wish you weren't gone so much. It's Sunday. Why can't you stay home?"

"I'll be back at five. Then I'll watch the boys while you go to the store. If I end up taking Caden to the bullfight, we won't leave 'til 6:30."

"Promise me none of the bulls will be hurt?"

"No, but I promise none of the bulls will be hurt on *purpose*."

"Wear your helmet."

"Sure." John washed down the last of his sandwich with a swallow of milk.

John's bike was custom-built to fit his six-foot-five-inch, two-hundred-pound frame. Ferrari orange with blue flames, chrome trim and stock Harley engine, the bike roared like a tiger, announcing John's arrival before you could see him. This usually worked in his favor because it, like every chopper, was pared down to its basic essentials, making it difficult to see him on the road.

April wasn't a fan of John's bike—and neither were his father and grandfather. "You have a wife and two babies," they often reminded him. "We'll buy the bike from you and keep it in storage until your family's a little older."

Eventually their reasoning succeeded. But John didn't want the bike languishing in storage somewhere. It needed to keep moving, just like John. Soon he would hand the keys over to the bike's new owner. But not before one last ride.

John's chopper was the third love of his life, with work and April vying for first. The victor depended on the day and the crisis at hand. Lately, work was prevailing, as a major business deal had been dominating his time. Fortunately, however, the transaction was almost completed. After half a year of hard work, the contracts were sitting on John's desk, waiting to be signed first thing the next morning.

But on this beautiful Sunday afternoon, John brokered a compromise between work and his immaculate chopper.

"I'll be back by five," John promised as he walked out the door, clad in a black sleeveless shirt, blue jeans and black Converse All Star tennis shoes.

April listened to the chopper engine roar to life and then fade away as her husband sped out of the neighborhood, his helmet still sitting on the floor next to the door to the garage.

*   *   *

Early that morning, Jan woke up with a strong compulsion to pray for her family. Still in bed, she spent time praying for each of her four children—Charles, Jennifer, John, and Jené—their spouses, and all nine of her grandchildren.

Once Jan felt at peace, she began her normal Sunday morning routine. A little later, Jan and James left for church. During the worship service, the guest preacher talked about the importance of encouragement. While he was speaking, Jan thought about John. *He's under so much pressure at work, he probably does need some encouragement.*

Suddenly, a vivid image came to her—an image of James and John walking up the twenty-three steps to the office of their family business. As they entered the front door, everyone in the office stood to their feet and gave John a standing ovation.

Driving home from church, Jan shared her vision-like experience with James, adding, "John works so hard. How can we make sure he feels encouraged and appreciated?"

"I'll mention it to him," James nodded. "In fact, it's a nice day; maybe I'll see if he's free for a round of golf. I can talk to him about it then."

When they got home, Jan changed out of her blouse and skirt into a pair of jeans and a flowery sleeveless top. James called John to see if he was free for golf.

"Not today, Dad. I'm on the chopper, and right now I'm at Store 416. Then I'm swinging by Erasmo's so he can follow me in his truck over to McCook. I want to take Caden to the bullfight tonight."

"Wait for me," James replied. "I'll fire up my bike and join you."

James threw on some jeans and a T-shirt. When he tried to start his motorcycle, he realized the battery was dead and called John back. "I won't be long," James promised. "Wait there and I'll head over as soon as I get it started."

"I'm going ahead. I'll ride slow and you catch up with me."

"That'll work," James consented. John never was one to stay still.

"Something to eat?" Jan asked her husband as he hung up the phone.

James shook his head. "I'll have to hurry if I'm going to catch up with John."

James and John had been riding motorcycles together since John was six. Jan loved that her husband got such enjoyment out of staying involved in the lives of all four of their kids and nine grandkids. Maybe it was because he grew up as an only child, but James got a lot of joy out of their big, close-knit family. It was one of the reasons he wanted all the kids working together with him in the family business.

Jan was still thinking about her family and counting her blessings when her thoughts were interrupted by her cell phone ringing in the other room. She answered it just before the call went to voicemail. When she did, she heard the voice of her daughter-in-law.

"Jan, this is April." The voice on the other end sounded tense.

*   *   *

Sunday afternoons in the Bible Belt are unlike anything north of the Mason-Dixon line. Like death and taxes, bumper-to-bumper traffic is a sure thing in even the smallest towns when churches are dismissed at high noon. Restaurants are packed with people wearing their Sunday best. And after lunch, they hit the malls and shopping centers.

Knowing that his beloved chopper would soon be gone, John savored their few remaining hours together. His bike was a stubborn relic from the carefree, unattached days of his youth. Since turning thirty-three six weeks earlier, he knew the time to grow up had finally arrived. He had already transitioned into what he thought it meant to be responsible. Working long hours. Driving hard deals. Focusing on his success. Providing for his family—even if it meant ignoring them in the process.

John pulled out of the Store 416 parking lot and turned north on Tenth Street. Knowing the speed limit was fifty-five miles per hour, he gunned the engine and slid into the inside lane, reveling in the feel of the wind in his hair. On his right, he passed a shopping center anchored by a Best Buy, Target, and Kohl's department store.

A silver Lumina pulled out of the shopping center parking lot to turn south on Tenth. Behind the wheel was a thirty-three-year-old woman accompanied in the car by her mother and young daughter.

Maybe John was traveling too fast on his streamlined chopper. Perhaps the stereo, inside the Lumina, drowned out the roar of the oncoming motorcycle. The police report says the driver turned her head to say something to her daughter in the backseat before pulling out into the street. Most likely, it was a combination of tragic factors that led to what happened next.

Pulling quickly onto Tenth to beat the oncoming southbound traffic, the woman never saw John at all.

The Lumina T-boned the chopper. The impact exploded the bike into six pieces, totaled the sedan and hurled John 150 feet—half the length of a football field—through the air. Spiraling over oncoming cars, his tailbone hit the asphalt first. The force of the landing slammed him backward, smashing his skull into the pavement. When John's body finally came to rest, he was laying on his back with his right leg twisted beside his head.

The woman driving the Lumina turned off the ignition, threw her face into her hands, and started to scream. "Oh my God, what have I done? What have I done?" Traffic in both directions came to a screeching stop. People left their cars and gathered, stunned, at the scene. Still conscious, John was thrashing about, trying to get up. He was bleeding from both ears and his nose.

As a man approached, John held out his cell phone and mumbled, "Call my wife—April." When John continued struggling to get up, another man held him still, while a woman knelt next to John and began to pray.

By now the first man had found April's number on speed dial. When a woman answered, he asked, "Is this April?"

"Yes—Who is this?"

"Ma'am, you don't know me, but your husband just handed me his cell phone and told me to call you. He's OK, but he's been in a motorcycle accident. A car hit him on Tenth and he hit his head on the pavement. I don't know if it's serious or not, but the ambulance should be here any minute, so you should probably go to McAllen Medical Center and wait for him there."

> "There's a good chance he won't be alive when we get there. I wouldn't rush getting ready for us if I were you."

April hung up her phone and thought to herself, *Mr. Tough Guy? He's indestructable. If they're sending him to the hospital it's probably just for observation.*

April called her mother to come over and watch the boys, and then she called Jan.

"John was hit by a car," April explained, trying to maintain composure, "but I'm sure it's not serious. They said an ambulance is on the way and we should go directly to the hospital."

Jan grabbed her car keys and ran for her husband. She found James in the carport trying to jump start his motorcycle.

At the scene of the accident, paramedic David Henrich knelt beside his partner, Paul Stevens, who was stabilizing the bloody head of the man on the asphalt. Wanting to assess how badly John was hurt, Henrich began asking a few questions.

John answered best he could, finally mumbling, "I think I'm OK, but my head and my hip really hurt."

Henrich peered to assess the wound. After swabbing the back of John's head with gauze, Henrich stood to his feet and walked several yards away before talking quietly into his walkie-talkie. "Transporting John Keller to McAllen Medical. Head injury. Doesn't look good."

With the help of two police officers, Stevens and Henrich moved John onto a gurney, secured his head to a cervical collar, and hoisted him into the ambulance. Climbing behind the wheel of the ambulance, Stevens called ahead to ER. "He's in shock right now and there's a good chance he won't be alive when we get there. I wouldn't rush getting ready for us if I were you."

While Stevens drove, Henrich started an intravenous solution of saline to replace the blood John had lost at the scene of the accident. He attached an EKG heart monitor to John's chest. Then he drew blood to run more tests. He took John's blood pressure and recorded the results on a clipboard.

Paramedics rarely sedate head injury victims because they need to perform continuous neuro checks, which they do by asking a battery of questions such as "Do you know what day today is?" "What's your name?" and "Where do you live?" But without sedation, John was hard to control. He kept pulling out his IV tube and heart monitor. Then he pushed Henrich away from the gurney and tried to stand up. Such behavior is common among people with brain injuries, as they often become agitated and confused. Twice Stevens had to pull the ambulance to the side of the road to help Henrich restrain their combative patient.

Erasmo was at home waiting for John to show up when April called with the news. On their way to the hospital, he and Maria passed the scene of the accident and saw a motorcycle lying in twisted pieces. Only one police car was left on the scene, but John's bike was easy to recognize. Tearing his eyes away and back onto the highway before him, Erasmo's jaw was hard and he inched the pedal closer to the floorboard.

As the ambulance pulled up to the entrance of the ER, Henrich saw a tight knot of people hovering by the double doors, waiting for John to arrive. He and Stevens pulled the gurney out of the back of the ambulance. As they wheeled their patient past his family, John's eyes were clenched shut and he was gritting his teeth under the tremendous pain.

During the admission intake inside the ER, Henrich approached the man he correctly assumed to be John's dad. "I saw your family praying when we pulled up," he said gently. "Just keep doing what you're doing. It doesn't look good. I'm afraid it'll be a miracle if your son lives."

If the determined look on James's face was any indication, this family was bolstered by a deep faith. Henrich was glad to see it. He suspected that John Keller was going to need all the help he could get.

3
Saving John

Two doctors approached the small mob milling about the emergency room waiting room. The shorter of the two cleared his throat, then spoke quietly into the steady drone of anxious voices.

"Excuse me, which one of you is April Keller?"

Close to thirty people filled the ER waiting area, all friends and family of the Kellers. Conversations ceased. Cell phones folded up. A hush of anticipation fell over the group.

"I'm April," a woman answered, stepping forward.

"I'm Doctor Nevaro. I'm the neurosurgeon on call." He extended a hand to April.

"And I'm Dr. Fulp, orthopedic surgeon," the second doctor said loudly with a slight cowboy drawl before extending his hand as well.

"Can we talk privately?" asked Dr. Nevaro.

April glanced at her father-in-law, then nodded.

Dr. Brian Nevaro and Dr. Trey Fulp were the top neurosurgeon and orthopedic surgeon, respectively, in the area. Besides their excellent reputations and similar ages, they seemed to have little in common. Nevaro was of medium build and soft-spoken. Fulp was an ex-Marine with a heart as big as his stature.

The doctors led April and James to John's room in the critical care unit. With a sheet pulled up over his body so that only his battered head was exposed, John looked like a corpse. He was laying perfectly still, his eyes closed, as blood slowly streamed out of nearly every orifice. His long body barely fitting on the bed, his feet poked out over the end. A nasogastric bag hung above his head, with a tube running into his nose.

April shuddered.

"He's under sedation," Dr. Nevaro said, "and we're still running tests to determine the extent of his injuries. What we *do* know is that his brain is hemorrhaging and swollen. Our goal is to stop the bleeding. To do that, we'll have to remove a section of his skull to access his brain. Because of the seriousness of John's head injury, time is limited. We'd like to operate immediately."

"We also know his pelvis is broken in three places," added Dr. Fulp. "Because he's hemorrhaging internally, we can't wait to repair the pelvis. We can wait a *little* longer to see if the brain is going to continue to swell. Or we can do both surgeries right now. What do you want us to do?"

"Both," April and James said at the same time.

April spoke around the aching lump in her throat. "How serious is—everything?"

"We can fix his pelvis," Dr. Fulp reassured her. "And his head, well, let's hope it's just a bump."

"With all due respect to Dr. Fulp, I don't want you to have unrealistic expectations," Dr. Nevaro interjected. "It'll take at least thirty-six hours—maybe as long as seventy-two—before we know the extent of the damage, but he's bleeding out of both ears, which means his brain is detached from the back of his skull, and that's serious."

He paused for a moment, and then looked directly at April. "We don't know how this is going to turn out for your husband," he said softly, "but I'm afraid there's a good chance he won't make it. And if he does, he'll likely be severely disabled the rest of his life."

"No, you don't understand," April said emphatically. "My husband is a strong man. He's going to be just fine!"

As the doctors turned to leave, Dr. Fulp looked at April and mouthed the words, "He'll be OK."

April turned to James. "Dr. Nevaro doesn't know John. If anyone can pull out of this, he can. He won't be satisfied until he does. If John can't go back to being the way he was, he won't want to be here."

"John's strong, April. And we're trusting God," James said. A moment later he added, "I'm going to find Jan and bring her on back. You OK here by yourself for a few minutes?"

April nodded.

Alone with John, April thought about the countless hours her husband spent every weekend meticulously working on his cars and his chopper. Caden enjoyed helping his daddy clean and polish the bike. When they were done, John usually rode the bike around the block to keep the battery charged. While Caden loved the chopper, he hated the loud noise it made when John fired it up.

> April whispered to John, "Your boys need a daddy and I need a husband. Work hard, John—you hear me?"

"This isn't the end," April whispered to John. "Your boys need a daddy and I need a husband. Work hard, John. Work on yourself just like you worked on your bike—you hear me?"

Later, after the family had been ushered out of John's room, an organ recovery team arrived to assess the situation. Recovery teams harvest organs and tissue after a patient has died for use as transplants to other patients. People with traumatic brain injuries are prime candidates for organ donations if the rest of their bodies are in relatively good condition, which was true in John's case. While organs and tissue can't be harvested without permission from the family, the team was already evaluating John as a potential donor.

Apparently, few people seemed to think that John would survive.

As afternoon turned to evening, other family members began to arrive. John's sister Jennifer and her family had been vacationing an hour away in the Rio Grande Valley when they got the news. Shortly after they got to the hospital, John's younger sister, Jené, and her family flew in from Dallas where they had been visiting family. John's brother, Charles, arrived from his home in Dallas as well on the same flight.

Friends flew in from all over Texas. John's best friend Robert, a corporal in the Army, was granted permission to fly home from Fort Bliss in El Paso. The moment he landed in McAllen, he organized a small team to pray for John every night from 10pm to 6am. Recruiting

Charles, Jené's husband, Jon, and Jennifer's husband, Rex, the four men agreed to faithfully gather to pray though the night for as long as John would be at McAllen Medical.

Five and a half hours later, the surgeries were over. Dr. Fulp met with the family. "I have good news," he said. "The surgery on John's pelvis was a success. I inserted three titanium pins—they're shaped like goal posts—to secure his pelvis. He should be ready to walk in a few days." He added, "I'm amazed that John's injuries aren't any worse, considering that he was thrown such a great distance in the air. He's obviously in very good shape."

"What difference would that make?" Jan asked.

"Strong muscles help prevent injury around the joints. And in a sudden impact, they help hold limbs together, preventing broken arms and legs."

Dr. Nevaro, however, delivered a more conservative report. "I removed a piece of John's skull—it's about the size of my hand—from the upper right quadrant to access the brain and stop the bleeding. I'm not putting the piece back yet because his brain is starting to experience some intracranial pressure. That means it's starting to swell. We need to give his brain room to expand."

"When will he wake up?" Jennifer asked.

"Right now, our goal is to keep him sedated until he stabilizes, which may take several days. Of course, there's still a very real danger you need to be aware of."

The family waited.

"We're not out of the woods yet. John sustained massive brain injuries. There's still a chance that he could drift into a coma. And if that happens," Nevaro added gravely, "all bets are off."

April faced a horde of challenges. Not only was she worried sick about John, she was also forced to think about a future without him. She loved being a stay-at-home mom for Dalton and Caden, but if John didn't survive, she knew she'd have to figure out a way to provide for herself and her children.

Then there were the daunting logistics of the present crisis. Her dad and stepmom were at her house, taking care of Dalton and Caden whenever she was at the hospital. Nevertheless, her sons still needed her. Still nursing the baby, every two to three hours she pumped milk for Dalton even when she was at the hospital. She also tried to spend a few hours with the boys every day, but the stress was taking a toll on the whole family.

In the meantime, the hospital staff was closely monitoring John's intracranial pressure (ICP), which is the pressure on the brain created

> Dr. Nevaro seemed somber—too somber for the good news he had just delivered. The family steeled themselves.

by swelling. Swelling can crush brain tissue, shift brain structures, contribute to hydrocephalus (also known as "water on the brain"), cut off the blood supply to certain parts of the brain and even cut off the blood supply to the brain altogether. If ICP rises too high or for too long, it can cause severe damage or even death.

John's ICP number fluctuated hourly as he lay sedated. Sometimes the nursing staff turned off his sedation medication to see if he would respond to stimulus. By applying sharp pressure to his fingernail, they were hoping he would jerk back to protect himself. Instead, he slowly drew his arms toward his body, indicating that his ICP was still high.

At 3:14 a.m. Tuesday morning, the night prayer team sent text messages to friends and family. The pressure in John's brain was climbing. Doctors intervened, administering an herbal drug called mannitol to relieve the swelling.

The next morning, the pressure on John's brain was down. In fact, his blood work looked so good that Dr. Nevaro began decreasing the sedation medication so that John could start to wake up. But on Wednesday, a CT scan revealed more bleeding in John's head. He was rushed into surgery again—his third in as many days. John's ICP spiked again.

After the surgery, Dr. Nevaro met with April, James and Jan. "We were able to stop the bleeding," he reported. But Nevaro seemed somber— too somber for the good news he had just delivered. The family steeled themselves.

"There's a high likelihood that the prolonged pressure has permanently damaged his brain. I'm sorry."

The room remained silent as Dr. Nevaro departed. After three relentless days of grasping for hope, cracks began appearing in the Keller family's armor.

Jan and April left to meet the rest of the family, with James to follow after he got in touch with the office. He had just pulled out his cell phone to text a message to Maria when Dr. Fulp stuck his head in the doorway. He was wearing scrubs, a cowboy hat and cowboy boots.

"Hey James, what say we go pay John a visit and pray for that 'little bump on his head'?"

A smile grew on James's face. "Your timing is impeccable. Let's go."

Dr. Fulp describes himself as a "simple redneck." The Kellers consider him a guardian angel. Gifted with an infectious smile that stretches from ear to ear, his love for people and his Texas-sized heart endear him to his patients.

And he's as committed to them as they are to him. When his patients are in crisis, he's been known to stay with them at the hospital for days at a time because he "forgot" to go home. Sometimes, his wife drives to the hospital to bring him a fresh supply of clean clothes.

Once James and Dr. Fulp entered John's room, they knelt beside the bed. Dr. Fulp began to pray. "Dear God, you know I've been at this for a long time—and I can't even begin to count how many patients I've seen since I started. Some didn't even make it out of surgery and some live very healthy lives today. But in all my life, I've never seen a family as committed to you as the Kellers. I've grown quite fond of them, Lord. It's not my place to tell you what to do, but I want to see a miracle for John. Would you do that for them—please? Amen."

By Friday morning, John's ICP numbers were higher than ever. John was hanging on by a thread. By noon, Dr. Nevaro operated on John once more to alleviate the pressure on his brainstem from the pools of blood.

On Saturday morning, John began stabilizing. His exhausted family hardly dared to ask each other the questions they longed to ask: Were they finally out of the woods? Was recovery finally within their grasp?

When Dr. Nevaro asked to meet with them that afternoon, no one was ready for what came next.

"John is no longer under sedation," Nevaro said, "so, I wanted to test his reflexes. I pinched John on his neck. No response. I pinched the other side of his neck. Still no response. I shined a flashlight in his eyes to check the dilation of his pupils. Nothing changed."

He paused and the air suddenly felt heavy.

"We've done everything we can, but John has slipped into a coma. There's nothing else we can do. Now we'll just have to wait."

Other words echoed in the room. They were the words Dr. Nevaro had spoken several days ago, after John's first brain surgery. Now his warning swirled around James and Jan and April, adding gravity to a situation that already felt hopeless:

"There's still a chance that John could drift into a coma. And if that happens, all bets are off."

4

Turtle Man

Eleven days after the accident, Jennifer had a vivid dream. In it, John was in a very dark place. Looking into the shadowy distance, John could see an open doorway and, beyond that, two small windows, which had voices emanating from behind them. John started walking toward the windows, and the voices grew louder; but because he was so far away, he found himself walking for a very long time. Eventually he reached the doorway and kept going. When he looked at the windows again, he saw that they belonged to two double doors, and that the light coming through them was sunlight. On the left side of the two doors was an elevator.

The next morning Jennifer, who was in McAllen, tried unsuccessfully to reach her mother to tell her about the strange dream.

Two days earlier, John had been transported by air to Houston. April's mom, a registered nurse, had flown with John in the twin engine plane from McAllen. Jan, James, April and Dalton—as well as John's best friend Robert—had followed. They would be joined soon by April's dad, stepmom and Caden.

The decision to move John from McAllen Medical Center to The Methodist Hospital in Houston had not been made lightly. John had gotten good care at the McAllen Medical Center, a five-hundred-bed hospital with a Level III trauma center rating. McAllen Medical had saved John's life, after all.

But now that John was in a coma, his family figured he needed the kind of resources available in a bigger city. The Methodist Hospital in Houston not only had those resources, but it was rated as a Level I trauma center. The choice seemed clear.

During John's first night at Methodist, doctors fitted him with a new pressure-reading device and a ventricular drain in his head.

The next morning, Dr. Ballard, the chief neurologist, informed John's family of what would happen next. "Our goal is to keep John alive and healthy until we can get him into a rehabilitation facility."

> As Jennifer described her strange dream about John, Jan started doodling. As Jennifer's dreamscape took shape on paper, Jan couldn't believe what she was seeing.

Jennifer reached her mother by phone a few hours later. As Jennifer described her strange dream about John, Jan picked up a piece of paper and started doodling the layout of the doors and windows that Jennifer had seen so vividly.

As Jennifer's dreamscape took shape on paper, Jan couldn't believe what she was seeing. "Jennifer!" she blurted, "You're describing John's room in the Neuro-Intensive Care Unit here at Methodist!"

"Mom," Jennifer said with tears in her eyes, "I think my dream means he's going to be OK. What I'm afraid of, though, is that it might take a very, very long time."

*   *   *

The families rented a two-bedroom apartment near the hospital. With April's family watching the boys, Jan and April spent every day and long into the evening with John. They prayed over him, talked to him, and helped the medical staff any way they could. James flew in every weekend after spending the week in McAllen running the business.

Sisters Jennifer and Jené continued faithfully posting updates to John's blog. When they added a hit-counter and map, they were astonished by what they discovered. Initially, visitors to the blog were limited to family and friends in Texas, as well as a handful of doctors and nurses from McAllen who wanted to keep up with John's progress. Soon, viewers shared the blog with their friends, and search engines began picking it up. Very quickly, people from all over the United States were following the blog and praying for John.

Meanwhile, the Methodist staff was doing their best to stabilize John. Day and night, John lay shivering on an arctic blanket to keep his brain from swelling further and to regulate his body temperature, something his injured brain could no longer do. In fact, his brain was no longer regulating several critical systems. Without intervention, John's temperature would rise unchecked, he would sweat profusely and his blood pressure and pulse would skyrocket. John had also been fitted with a trach and feeding tube. And to complicate things further, he'd come down with double pneumonia.

On one particularly horrible day, Dr. Ballard took an EEG to measure electrical activity—and found much less brain activity than expected. He told the family, "The results don't give me much hope for him to wake up. And even if he does wake up, he's likely to be bedridden or spend the rest of his life in a wheelchair."

Despite the discouraging EEG, none of the doctors were willing to deny that miracles can happen. And the Kellers continued believing for that miracle.

Three weeks to the day after John's accident, the first glimmers of progress occurred. When the father of one of John's college roommates came to visit, he was holding John's hand when James said, "Hey, Son, why don't you squeeze Roy's hand?" To the astonishment of both men, John did just that.

Another day, when a doctor entered John's room and called out, "Hey John!" John jumped as if he'd been startled.

Eventually, the physical therapists were able to get John to sit without falling over in a reclining bed, and then in a chair. Pleased with John's progress, Dr. Ballard recommended that he be transferred to TIRR Memorial Hermann (TIRR) in Houston, one of the top rehabilitation hospitals in the nation.

The day before he was transferred to TIRR, John squeezed his dad's hand three times when asked.

* * *

"I have good news," a nurse announced to Jan and April as they walked to John's room on the morning of his first day at TIRR. "John is going to be staying in Room 310."

"Why is that good news?" Jan asked.

"That's the room we call the 'Miracle Room.' Miracles happen there all the time. The last patient who stayed in that room spent four months there. His wife and ten-month-old son spent every day with him. By the time he left, he was walking and talking. His family asked me to make sure whoever stayed here next knew it was the Miracle Room."

"It's the perfect room, then," Jan smiled. "We believe God is going to work a big miracle in John's life and that he'll be restored completely."

> One of the first things they did was Scotch-tape John's eyes open to stimulate his brain.

"Well, we see miracles all the time around here," the nurse said. "I'll be working with a patient who is asleep, and suddenly that patient will wake up and start reading my name tag out loud."

It was exactly what the family needed to hear.

TIRR's "Wake John" campaign was the most aggressive yet. Every day, the staff dressed John in workout clothes (no more hospital gowns!), moved him into a wheelchair, and kept him active from eight in the morning until five in the afternoon.

One of the first things they did was Scotch-tape John's eyes open to stimulate his brain. Then, they went to extreme measures—even putting coffee grounds in his mouth and pulling the hair on his arms—trying to get him to respond even if it was out of repulsion, frustration or pain.

One of John's physical therapists recommended they do anything within reason to aggravate him. So he brought a water gun into John's hospital room and squirted him in the face. Another morning he walked into the room with a bucket of ice. He held ice against John's face, under his armpits, even dropped some down his pants.

But John never moved.

John was on a feeding tube. He wore diapers. He couldn't make eye contact or talk or even nod. Plus, he was suffering from the effects of abnormal posturing: arms curled in toward his chest, hands clenched into fists, legs extended with his feet pointed away from his body.

Abnormal posturing occurs when damage to the central nervous system causes the muscles to involuntarily contract or extend. This usually indicates damage in the parts of the brain that control consciousness, sleep, alertness, thinking, speaking and memory.

Hospital staffers told the Kellers that John's case of abnormal posturing was the worst they had ever seen.

The condition can't be fixed by simply bending the body into a normal position. Instead, the brain needs to heal and the muscles and tendons need to be massaged until they become flexible again.

Therapists exercised John's arms and legs to prevent atrophy and spasticity from setting in, and April worked right along with them day after day. After therapy sessions, she frequently continued working with John on his range of motion. She was tireless, often telling the therapists, "I want my husband back just the way he was!"

April's drive to get John back just the way he was gave her a lot of strength. But was it setting her up for heartbreak? Time would tell.

Dr. Fulp happened to be in Houston and decided to pay John a visit. The good doctor entered the hospital room and walked up to his former patient's bed, ignoring Jan who was knitting and April who was reading a book.

"John, you might not remember me but my name is Trey Fulp and I'm the doctor who put your pelvis back together about the same time you earned that little bump on your head. I'm so glad to see you're alive. I'll tell you what. Just so I can be sure that you're alive, why don't you blink your eyes for me?"

With his eyes still closed, John fluttered his eyelids in a blinking motion.

Dr. Fulp waved Jan and April over and gestured excitedly toward John's face. Then he continued talking with a calm voice. "That was good, John. But this time, would you blink twice for me?"

John fluttered his eyes twice.

"Now move your mouth."

John moved his mouth.

"John is a miracle!" Fulp laughed out loud. "I can't believe what I'm seeing! He's a miracle!"

Within a few days, John began opening his eyes just a slit. During one session, a therapist clapped loudly in front of his face, causing him to flinch. The doctors conducted an optic nerve study and determined that John's eyes had suffered no damage, meaning it was reasonable to think that if he woke up he would be able to see. His eyes began dilating, which meant he could be close to waking up.

In order to get John ready to stand, his physical therapists laid him flat on an incline table. They raised the table ten degrees and measured his blood pressure and respirations to monitor the stress on his body. His vital signs were good, so they increased the incline. Again, he was fine, so they increased it again. Within a half hour, John was at a 60 percent incline.

> The side of John's head looked like an underinflated basketball, with one side noticeably caved in.

Jan, who had been watching the progress, couldn't stay quiet another minute. "This is good, right?"

"It's really, *really* good," one of the physical therapists replied. "Usually patients can only endure about ten minutes their first day and definitely don't make it to sixty degrees. Lot of times, patients throw up because of the stress on their body. But your son's doing great!"

During another therapy session, John was placed on the incline board at sixty degrees. The angle naturally prompted him to raise his head slightly off the board. The therapists were talking and laughing among themselves, which piqued Jan's curiosity.

"What's so funny?" she asked.

"Well," one of them answered, "in our morning meeting, we were betting whether or not John would be able to hold his head up at this incline for thirty seconds. Right now he's going on seven minutes."

One day, John started making noises. Not words, but noises. It was a start.

About that time, doctors decided that John had officially come out of his coma. Their criteria was that, when asked, John could respond by opening his eyes, even if just a slit.

After being comatose for seventy days, John's condition was upgraded to "minimally conscious."

While the family celebrated the news, they knew they were just beginning the journey. While John sometimes responded to stimuli or questions, he couldn't talk or walk or even hold his head upright. His legs and feet were still locked straight, his arms continued to curl to his chest, and his hands remained frozen and crab-like.

The side of John's head looked like an underinflated basketball, with one side noticeably caved in where Dr. Nevaro had removed a piece of his skull during that very first emergency surgery. While skin and hair covered the hole, nothing else protected his brain in that spot. His head hung forward most of the time, and his eyes were unfocused. If someone were to lift John's face in their hands and look into his eyes, they couldn't say for sure that he saw them in return, or if he was even there.

One afternoon, April brought baby Dalton to the hospital room and sat him on John's lap.

"Why don't you give Dalton a kiss, John?"

Ever so slowly, John began lowering his head. The family watched in awe. Eventually he lowered his head enough to rest his lips on Dalton's head.

About that time one of the physical therapists walked into the room. With tears in her eyes, Jan pointed to John, whose lips were still resting on Dalton's head, and said, "Marci, this is what we're talking about. He's in there. I know he's in there."

KELLER HOME VIDEO
"Kiss the Baby"
Scan with smartphone or visit
vitalconnectionsbook.com

Two days after John "kissed" Dalton, April wanted to bring Caden to see John. She hadn't brought him sooner because she'd been trying shield him from seeing John at his worse, which is why Caden hadn't seen his daddy in three months, not since the morning of the accident. April knew they needed to be reunited. Still, she was nervous about how Caden would react to seeing his dad semicomatose.

"April, honey, bring Caden to the hospital and I'll meet you both downstairs," Jan offered. "Then you go on ahead so you're waiting for us in John's room, and I'll walk Caden on up." Jan suspected there was a better chance of Caden taking the whole thing in stride if he didn't pick up on his mother's nervousness. April agreed.

As Jan and Caden walked hand-in-hand toward the elevators, they passed by the hospital gym. Having heard the grownups talk about his dad's workouts, Caden said matter-of-factly, "That's Daddy's gym." In the elevator, Caden got to push the button to the third floor. As they walked down the hallway, Caden held a Matchbox Jeep in one hand, and his grandma's hand in the other.

As soon as Jan opened the door to John's room, Caden walked right up to the bed and raised his arms to be lifted onto the mattress. April gave him the boost he wanted. He climbed on top of his dad and ran his Jeep back and forth across John's chest.

> Caden raised his arms. April gave him the boost he wanted. He climbed on top of his dad and ran his Jeep back and forth across John's chest.

Jan had already prepared him for the fact that his daddy couldn't talk, and Caden seemed to want to let the women know he understood. "It's OK," he told them reassuringly, "Daddy no talk."

Caden saw that his dad had a sore on his nose from where an oxygen mask had rubbed away the skin. As he and his grandma got ready to leave, he asked to see his daddy's doctor. In the hallway, Jan found one of the doctors; Caden told him to give his daddy a Band-Aid for his nose.

The whole thing had gone better than expected.

What was heartbreaking, however, was the response from John. There was nothing. Not a single movement, blink or gesture.

Saying John had come out of his coma was like saying the train was out of the tunnel when only the engine had exited while the rest of the railroad cars were following behind in the darkness. There was still so much farther to go.

One afternoon, April was visiting John, telling her unresponsive husband about something cute one of the boys had done, when something about John's face caught her attention. Looking closer, she saw a tear running down his cheek.

A glimmer of light may have appeared, but John was still very much in the dark.

*   *   *

One day the Kellers got news that their health insurance company thought John's improvements were too incremental to continue paying for him to stay at TIRR.

April and Jan began searching for another facility that would admit John. Call after call, they were rebuffed. "He's too high-maintenance for our staffing level" they were told. Finally, they began calling nursing homes and John was accepted at University Place Nursing Center, a skilled-nursing facility that typically works with senior citizens who are rehabilitating from surgery or a stroke.

When they walked into University Place for the first time, April thought to herself, *This looks like the land that time forgot!* The facility was top-notch, but John seemed a third of the age of the rest of the patients.

April and Jan followed as John was wheeled into his new room. They met his new roommate—an eighty-year-old man watching the news with the volume turned as high as it could go. The room had no wheelchair, no shower, and a small bathroom. The bed was far too short for John's six-foot-five frame.

After getting him settled, April snuck away to the bathroom and cried.

While the Keller clan was grateful that UP had admitted John, the move felt like a huge setback.

That weekend, James flew in from McAllen. Walking into John's room, he knelt down on one knee beside his son and spoke quietly but firmly into his ear.

"John, you look good."

John didn't respond.

"Son, you look better, feel better, talk better, walk better, smell better, taste better, eat better. You *are* better today than you were yesterday."

> Something caught April's attention. Looking closer, she saw a tear running down John's cheek.

After that, every time James visited his son, he repeated the same words. Over and over again. Despite the fact that John never responded or looked any different than he had the last time his dad was there.

An intern complained about it to one of the doctors. "I don't understand why he keeps telling John he's better," she said. "We don't even know how much John can understand, plus he's offering his son false hope."

"Leave him alone," the doctor admonished. "Just because John isn't responding to his father's words doesn't mean he can't hear or understand what he's saying."

> Someone had posted a sign above John's bed in the middle of the night: "John Keller—Miracle in Progress."

While John was at University Place, doctors made plans to cover the hand-sized hole in John's skull with a custom-made Titanium piece, permanently sealing the gap that Dr. Nevaro had left in place three months earlier to accommodate the swelling of John's brain.

Every time John went into surgery, his family's greatest fear was that he wouldn't wake back up. He was far from fully awake, but at least he was responding in small ways. What if they couldn't get him to wake back up even that much?

But closing the hole in John's head had to happen sooner or later.

Before the surgery, the staff weaned John off neurostimulants he'd been on to stimulate his brain. The surgery went well, and as the anesthesia wore off, John seemed much more relaxed and responsive. Within a few weeks, his abnormal posturing began subsiding. Soon his arms were no longer coiling up next to his chest.

Because his arms had loosened up, therapists and family members started working with him on an arm bike—essentially a tabletop bicycle pedaled with the hands. They also laid John on his stomach for a variety of exercises, which stretched out his chest muscles. Soon, he could wiggle his toes on command. Not long after that, he began touching his chin and nose on command!

While John was making progress in many areas, he wasn't tracking things with his eyes. Most of the time, he had a blank, deer-in-the-headlights look.

Jan and April worked with John daily, prying open his stiff crab-like hands, stretching his arms, and massaging his muscles. They massaged his legs, flexed his knees, and worked his toes.

Because John's body had been impacted so long by the abnormal posturing, the tendons in his legs and toes were extremely tight, making walking impossible. Doctors operated yet again, cutting and lengthening his tendons so he could get back the range of motion he had lost. Afterward, one of the surgeons met with Jan. "John did great in surgery," he told her. "No complications whatsoever. Now we just wait for him to wake up."

But John wasn't waking up.

From the chair beside his bed, Jan waited. She tried shaking his shoulder. She prayed for him. She threw cold water on his face. Still no response.

As she sat in John's eerily silent room, her cell phone rang. Her caller ID told her it was April, who was at the apartment that night with the boys.

"Jan, I have an idea," April said. "Caden's been praying for his daddy to wake up, so I thought, why don't we put him on the phone and see what happens?"

"Anything's worth a try," Jan replied.

As Jan held the cellphone to John's ear, Caden began yelling, "Daddy wake up! Daddy, wake up! Daddy, wake up!"

John's eyes began twitching, then blinking, and then they opened.

A few mornings later, Jan arrived at John's room and read a sign above his bed that a tech had posted in the middle of the night: "John Keller—Miracle in Progress."

It was so very true.

*　　　*　　　*

In early October, John's insurance company approved his return to TIRR. He'd been away for nearly four months. The homecoming he received from the staff was filled with cheers, hugs, and pats on the back. He was even assigned to Room 310—the Miracle Room—once again.

The therapists soon found a way for John to communicate with them. They gave him a pen and taught him how to click once for "yes" and twice for "no."

One day April wheeled John outside. It was a beautiful day and she wanted to enjoy it with him. On a whim she said, "John, I want to see how well you can write. Can you write 'hi'?" She put a notebook on his lap.

Clutching his pen with stiff curled fingers, he painstakingly scrawled the word "hi."

April immediately picked up her cell phone and called Jan.

"You won't believe what John just did! I asked him to write 'hi' on a piece of paper...and he did it!"

After that, John continued scrawling answers to questions. Sometimes, however, no one could read his handwriting, and would ask him to try again. And again. Frustrated, John would underline his scribbles over and over as if saying, "Please understand me!!"

One exasperating afternoon, April blurted, "John, I'm sorry I can't read your writing. Can you just nod your head for 'yes' and shake your head for 'no'?"

She looked into his eyes and under her breath prayed, *Lord, please let him respond.*

John nodded.

April couldn't believe what she'd just seen! Brimming with excitement, she asked John a volley of questions. Then she wheeled him to the gym where his occupational therapist was working.

"Laurie!" April exclaimed. "Watch this! John, are the San Antonio Spurs going to win the NBA Finals finals this year?"

John shook his head.

"How about the Mavericks? Are the Dallas Mavericks going to win the NBA finals?"

John nodded his head.

Eight long months after his accident, John and April were communicating! He had started by blinking his eyes, then clicking a pen, then scrawling a few words, and finally nodding. It was almost too good to be true!

In order to prepare John to walk, the therapists placed him on a stationary bike. When they determined his feeble legs were strong enough, they placed him in a standing frame. Then they put him in a standing harness behind a walker. Even though it took four people to hold his arms in place, steady his head and move his legs, John's advancement to a walker represented huge progress.

While relearning to walk, John would grow tired and try to sit down. In the consummate battle of wills, April would walk in front of him while the therapist followed directly behind him. Whenever John tried to sit, April would hold him up and the therapist would place his knees behind John's knees—catching him in his lap—and refuse to sit down.

Amazingly, John was soon speeding up and down the hallways with his walker.

The same determination that created a chiseled workout king before the accident was kicking in and motivating John to improve.

As his legs grew stronger, John—while still belted into his wheelchair—began standing and shuffling several steps while holding onto the metal rail in the corridor. Nurses and staff shook their heads at the spectacle of a semicomatose patient shuffling brief distances along the wall with a wheelchair strapped to his back like a shell. The staff began calling him "Turtle Man."

While John was making tremendous strides, he was still only partially awake. And he still wasn't talking.

*   *   *

With Christmas around the corner, the doctors gave John permission to leave TIRR and spend a few hours with his family.

But before he could leave the rehab center—even for a few hours—there was much for John's family to do and learn. Staff members patiently taught John's family how to get him in and out of a wheelchair. They taught John how to hold onto the top of the open passenger door, and then lower himself into the car while Jan helped him swing his feet inside. He even remembered how to buckle his seat belt.

After one such practice session, Jan told her son, "I'm so proud of you! You should have no problem on Christmas Day. Now let's get you back upstairs." As she reached to unbuckle John's seat belt, he pushed her hand away roughly and grunted. Thinking his arm had randomly spasmed, she tried to unbuckle him again. Again he pushed her hand away and grunted.

By now John's face had turned beet red. Jan realized he was angry. "I'm sorry, Son, but we were just practicing getting you in and out of the car. It's not time for you to leave the hospital quite yet."

Jan and a few nurses tried to pry John out of the car, but he refused to cooperate. Finally, they left him alone for fifteen minutes so he could cool down. Jan could understand John's increasing frustration with being confined to his room and his uncommunicative body.

> As they drove into the parking lot, John started groaning. They weren't groans of pain. John was angry.

On Saturday morning, John appeared alert and excited about leaving the premises and celebrating Christmas. His family successfully got him out of his wheelchair and into the car. With wide eyes, John watched the landscape whizzing by. Freedom!

James brought lunch from Lupe Tortillas, the TIRR staff's favorite Mexican restaurant in Houston. Even though John relied on a feeding tube in his abdomen for nutrition, the family gave him a few bites of Mexican food to roll around in his mouth. He savored every bite.

After lunch, they moved John out of his wheelchair and onto the couch. There was plenty of commotion from the barrage of conversations and kids running around the two-bedroom apartment. John watched everything wide-eyed; and, when he was asked if he wanted to rest, he shook his head no.

As they sat in a circle unwrapping gifts, April opened a present for John. "Look, a bottle of cologne!" she said.

Since the brain injury, John had no sense of smell. Still, he took the bottle of cologne in stiff hands and tried to open it. His sister Jené relieved him of the job, opened the bottle and splashed cologne on his face and neck.

At the end of the day, April looked at her watch. "It's been a long day. We probably need to get John back." Jennifer and Jené cleaned up the living room while Charles washed the dishes. Jan and April gathered John's things. John didn't understand what was happening in that moment.

"Let's get you back in your wheelchair," James said. James grabbed John's hand and helped him stand up from the couch. Then he positioned him to sit down in the wheelchair. James and Jan agreed to drive John back to TIRR.

As they drove into the hospital parking lot, John started groaning. They weren't groans of pain; they were groans that communicated John was angry. After James parked the car, Jan got out and opened the passenger door.

"We need to get you out," she said to John.

John shook his head and groaned. His face turned beet red, as it had during their practice session. Jan tried unbuckling his seat belt, and, again, he roughly swatted her hand away.

James put his hand on Jan's shoulder and leaned in toward their son. He spoke kindly but firmly.

"I know you don't want to go back into that hospital—and we don't want to take you back, either. But you're not ready to leave yet. You probably have another month here before we can move you back home. Once you can walk out of here on your own, without anyone helping you, we'll go home to McAllen. But it's not going to be tonight. I'm sorry, Son."

Tears streamed down John's face. After several minutes of silence, John held out his hand so his dad could pull him out of the car. James held his son in his arms and whispered in his ear, "You look better, feel better, talk better, walk better, smell better, taste better, eat better. You are better today than you were yesterday. And very soon, you'll come home."

In his hospital bed that night, John sorted through the cobwebs in his mind, trying to remember his earlier life. During the eleven months since the accident, it felt like someone had been ever so gradually turning up the lights with a dimmer switch. At first, after he started coming out of that initial seventy-day coma, he felt like he was laying at the bottom of a swimming pool. People were hovering overhead, but he couldn't make sense of what they were saying or doing. Slowly, he rose to the surface and began to understand.

Laying in bed, John stared at a nightlight at the other side of the room. His world looked as if he were peering through the wrong end of a pair of binoculars.

Ever so faintly, John remembered how it felt to walk. To play basketball with Caden. To hold Dalton in his arms. What life was like beyond the walls of hospital after hospital. He wanted his freedom back. The inner resolve that had once created a star athlete and driven businessman stirred inside John. Somewhere inside, he grew determined to break free from his mental and physical prison.

The next morning, John seemed to have a renewed focus. During physical therapy, his therapist placed three laundry detergent bottles in front of him. They were filled with water, each one heavier than the last. John bent over, grabbed the handle of the first bottle and lifted it high over his head. He set the bottle on the floor and repeated the same thing with the second bottle. Then he moved to the third bottle. This time, he didn't just hold the heaviest bottle over his head—he pumped it up and down several times above his shoulders like it was a dumbbell.

He moved to the weight machine and was instructed to raise the weight as many times as possible. He bench-pressed the weight ten times and then stopped to catch his breath. Then he bench-pressed the weight ten more times. He counted the repetitions silently in his mind, which impressed the therapists.

John's determination was epic. He wouldn't rest, even at night. He would climb out of bed and crawl, like a baby, to the chair. Then he would crawl back and forth repeatedly. He even slept with his tennis shoes on to get better traction. His brain was firing, and though he

> Immediately John shook his head and grunted. He thought he was going home with his dad. James tugged at John's arm, but he refused to budge.

wasn't quite sure where he was or what he was doing, he was certainly determined to keep it up!

Afraid he would fall out of bed and hurt himself, the nursing staff eventually moved John's mattress to the floor. When he appeared anxious and seemed to need a lot of reassuring, Jan began sleeping next to him on the floor.

By New Year's Day, John was dedicating every available minute toward his rehabilitation. "I'm truly amazed at what John is doing," one doctor commented. Another said, "After looking at his CT scan, I didn't expect to see him so awake and alert." Another doctor predicted, "John'll be talking before the anniversary of his accident."

That first week in January, the Kellers and John's doctors decided that John could be discharged on January 31—if he could build the stamina to walk by himself by then.

The next week, John appeared to be staggering as he walked. The doctors tested him, but he refused to cooperate. As he became increasingly irritable and aggressive, the staff began restraining him. This only made matters worse. John had an irrepressible urge to move and keep moving. If he tried to go somewhere and got stopped by a locked door, he would get angry and begin kicking the door.

John's change in behavior came as no surprise to the doctors—aggressive behavior is common among patients with traumatic brain injuries. As one doctor explained to the family, "John has lost the filter in his brain that tells him how to treat people."

On Monday, January 19, James arrived from McAllen for a visit. Holding John's arm, he helped him walk outside, then handed him a basketball.

"Let's see what you got," he said with a grin.

Twelve times, John threw the ball in the direction of the basket before he ran out of steam. The two sat down at a bench beside the court. John had already worked up a sweat.

"Once you catch your breath, I'll take you back to your room," James said.

Immediately, John shook his head and grunted. He thought he was going home with his dad. When it was time to go, James tugged at John's arm, but he refused to budge.

"Look," James said, "you want to go home; we want you home. But you only have ten more days here. It may seem like a lifetime before you leave, but look—you're thirty-four years old. Ten days is nothing compared to thirty-four years. The time will go by much quicker if you cooperate and take it easy on the staff. Can you do that for yourself and for me, too?"

John didn't respond, but James hoped that he understood. After a few minutes of cooling down, the two walked back to John's room.

That Wednesday, a new occupational therapist walked into John's room and introduced herself. She spoke with a British accent which made her seem a little out of place compared to the many other staff members whose voices reflected the southern states they hailed from. As she acquainted herself with John, Jan walked into the room.

"John, who is that?" the new therapist asked.

John looked over his shoulder at his mother. Then he said, "Mom."

It wasn't a cough or a grunt. His voice sounded raspy, like he was suffering from laryngitis, but it was unmistakable. John had spoken his first word in 344 days!

Jan's eyes welled up with tears. "Look, Son, there it is. You found your voice. If you can say that, say 'Praise the Lord!'"

"Praise the Lord!" John said.

"Do you know where you are?" the therapist asked.

John shook his head.

"John," his mother said, "you've been in the hospital here in Houston for almost a year. You were in a serious motorcycle accident and had a traumatic brain injury."

John wrinkled his forehead. "April?"

"She's in McAllen for a few days with your boys, Dalton and Caden."

John asked about his dad and siblings. He wanted to know about the family business. Most of all, he was shocked that almost a year had transpired since the accident.

"Let's call April," Jan said.

Jan called April's number on her phone. When April answered, Jan said, "John wants to speak to you." April was confused. What was her mother-in-law talking about?

John grabbed the phone from his mother. "Hello?"

"John!!" April screamed. "You can talk! You can talk!"

April pelted John with questions without even taking a breath for him to answer.

Finally, as she paused to inhale, John stammered, "April, I love you."

"I love you too!" April cried.

The moment they hung up, John looked at his mom.

"I need to call Dad."

James was driving back to McAllen from Houston with his son-in-law Jon. When his phone rang, he could see on the caller ID that the call was coming from Jan.

"Yeah, honey."

"Dad, it's me—John."

James didn't know what to say. Tears blurred his vision as he drove in silence.

"Dad, are you there?"

"John, it's so good to hear your voice, Son."

"Dad, I'm doing great. I'm here with Mom. I started talking today, and I just had to call you, Dad, and tell you that I love you."

At that point, James couldn't say anything because he was crying so hard. He handed the phone to Jon and pulled over to the side of the road so he wouldn't cause an accident.

John spent the rest of the afternoon calling family and friends to let them know their prayers were answered. Amazingly, he could recall every phone number by memory.

As afternoon turned to evening, Jan reclaimed her phone. She needed to get something to eat. "Honey, why don't you take a break while I go eat dinner? You can make more calls when I get back."

After Jan left, a nurse entered John's room to check on him.

"Can I use your phone?" he asked. "I need to call my friends."

She stopped and looked at him. "What if I don't have a cell phone?"

"Everyone has a cell phone," he retorted.

She folded her arms for a moment before reaching into her pocket and handing over her phone.

TIRR had done good. John Keller was awake.

On January 29, John put on sweat pants and a T-shirt with a verse from the Bible printed on the back:

Looking unto Jesus the author and finisher of our faith; who for the joy that was set before him endured the cross, despising the shame, and is set down at the right hand of the throne of God. Hebrews 12:2

This verse had given hope to John's family as they held tightly—for almost a year—to the belief that John's life wasn't finished yet, and that Jesus would give him the strength to complete this leg of his journey.

Then, accompanied by the applause and cheers of staff and family, John walked out of TIRR on his own power. He was going home.

His first destination was his parents' home in McAllen. For the time being, John would live with them. Everyone agreed that, with a one-year-old and three-year-old at home, April's hands were full, and John still needed constant supervision and considerable care. He was being fed through a tube, he needed diapers, his hands were curled, he couldn't hold his head upright and he was on eighteen different medications. On top of all that were issues with his memory, social filters, reasoning, vision and more.

While John loved and missed his family, he was a long way from reassuming the role of husband to April or father to Dalton and Caden.

In many ways, he was a child trapped in an adult's body.

5

Homeward Bound

Two weeks before John came home, Jan got a call from Rick Vasquez, a technician who had worked with John during his physical therapy at TIRR. Rick had recently moved from Houston to McAllen, and was calling to see how John was doing.

During the conversation, Rick mentioned that while he enjoyed his current job working with kids, he missed working with adults.

"How would you feel about working with John again?" Jan asked.

Rick loved the idea. When John arrived at his parents' home, he was greeted by a newly installed garage gym as well as his own personal rehab technician.

Because John still needed help walking, Rick worked on building John's stamina. In addition to working out in the garage gym, they walked the neighborhood. They walked through the local mall. John also walked the treadmill for up to three hours a day.

The more John walked, the stronger he became.

A week after arriving home, John felt strong enough to pay a visit to the office. One year and three weeks after Jan's vision of John walking up the twenty-three steps into the office of the family business, he did it. Because he was still weak, he took his time climbing the stairs. But when he walked through the front door, everyone in the office stood to their feet and gave him a standing ovation.

John walked into his old office, sat down at his computer, and remembered his password to log in. He could also remember which reports he'd been working on right before the accident.

What John simply could not remember was anything new. He never knew where he'd left his cell phone, wallet or even the car keys he wasn't allowed to use but insisted on carrying nevertheless. And because he couldn't remember what he'd said ten minutes earlier he would repeat himself incessantly. He couldn't even remember when he last visited the bathroom so he went three or four times every hour (hoping to avoid an accident in the dreaded diapers he still wore). To make matters even *more* complicated, he could never remember how to find the bathroom, even in his parents' house, even after he had been living there for several weeks.

> April held back stinging tears. This wasn't her husband at all. He was as much a child as Caden.

Why could John remember things from before the accident, but not what he'd done or said ten minutes ago?

John could remember things he learned and did before the accident because healthy cognitive skills had processed and moved those things securely into his memory bank.

After the accident, however, his damaged cognitive skills simply couldn't get new information where it needed to be. Before that could ever change, John would need to rebuild vital neural connections and get damaged cognitive skills up and running again.

* * *

"John!" April hissed. "You can't do that."

They were standing in the cereal aisle at Walmart. April was holding Dalton, who was screaming. Caden, sitting in the cart, was whining tearfully as well.

John had asked a woman buying corn flakes if she owned a motorcycle. It was how he always initiated conversations with strangers. Now he was several minutes into a monologue about his accident. He was at the part where he was flying through the air like a helicopter. No longer grasping the concept of personal space, he was practically standing on the woman's toes. She did not look happy.

"John," April tried again, "we have to go. The kids are tired and hungry."

"No, I have to tell my story."

April tried to smile at the woman. "John, this nice woman has shopping to do. And we need to go. Let's go."

"Why?" He demanded. "Why won't you let me tell my story?"

They eventually made it to the car. Driving John to his parents' house, April held back stinging tears. She had been so ready to have her husband back. But this wasn't her husband at all. He was as much a child as Caden. Except when her three-year-old threw a tantrum, April could handle it. When a six-foot-five-inch man threw a tantrum, it was an entirely different matter altogether.

Despite the growing tension between John and April, that spring John began transitioning home with April and the boys. He started by spending the night one or two times a week. By fall, he had moved back in.

The changes were difficult on everyone.

Bewildered, April told her mom, "The person who came home from the hospital isn't the man I married. Actually, it's like having a third child, and I have no idea how to handle that. I want to be a wife to him, but instead I'm his therapist, mom and nurse. I don't know how to transition us back to husband and wife."

John was overwhelmed, too. Living in a house with two kids creates a level of commotion that falls somewhere between delightful and tolerable for most people. For someone with a TBI, however, it can be excruciating. John's brain was so overstimulated by the normal sounds of family life that he couldn't sleep at night. And with his limited vision, he was constantly tripping over toys and even his own children. Life with his wife and sons had become a minefield of chaos and tension.

Because John's brain injury had impacted his logic & reasoning as well as his ability to regulate his reactions, he was prone to outbursts. One day he lost his temper. He grabbed a paint stir stick and whacked the treadmill to let Caden know he was upset. The wooden stick broke in two as Caden, terrified, ran to his mother.

After that, John moved back in with his parents. He'd lived at home with April and the boys for three months. Whether or not he would return was the burning question no one could answer.

*   *   *

"Caden, where are you? Are you still here? Say something, Caden." There was frustration in John's voice.

Jan bit her lip and watched from the doorway as John felt his way around the family room furniture trying to find his three-year-old. In the meantime, Caden, gripping a candy bar in each hand, stayed just beyond John's reach and his line of sight. It's easy, after all, to evade someone with tunnel vision—and blurry tunnel vision at that.

"No! I don't wanna say anything!" Caden yelled in defiance, giving John the edge he was looking for. Turning toward Caden's voice, he spotted his son and tried to grab hold of him, coming up empty-handed.

At that point, John gave in. He made his way back to the computer on the desk next to the couch, grabbed the mouse, leaned in close to the monitor, and clicked on the button that said RESUME GAME.

Caden had won again, this time with less screaming than usual. Today's prize was a couple of candy bars. He retreated to the opposite side of the room, folded his legs beneath him, and ate not one but both candy bars in record time. Not that he needed to worry. John was absorbed in the game on the computer. Apparently he was done being a dad for the day.

That night while they were getting ready for bed, Jan told James what she'd seen, then lamented, "John's getting more lackadaisical as a parent every day. I know we said he needs to do this on his own, but he can't even tell the boys to go to bed without forgetting what he just told them! They know that if they just stall for a bit, they won't have to do anything their daddy tells them to do. And on top of all that, half the time he can't even see them! I wish there was a way to improve his memory, and his eyesight, too."

"It's also about confidence," James added. "John doesn't believe anymore that he can be a good dad."

But in addition to all the struggles, John's folks were seeing something good emerging out of the gloom of John's TBI: a warm, funny side of

John's personality that they hadn't seen in years. Probably not since he was a kid. Sometimes his parents would marvel at the differences they saw.

"Remember how curt he used to be in meetings?" Jan said.

James nodded. "Or how he was too busy to ever grab lunch?"

"And he was so matter-of-fact!" Jan added. "No chit chat, no 'How you doing?' or 'What's going on in your life?' He's sure not like *that* anymore!"

James grinned. "See? There's progress right there."

*   *   *

After seeing something on TV about a company called Lumosity®, Jan wondered if their digital brain training programs could improve John's memory.

"They have computer games that are supposed to exercise your brain," she explained to James one day while they were in the garage watching John complete a set of bicep curls.

"John loves games," James said. "It's certainly worth a try."

They signed up. The first game John played featured birds with dots on their backs. John was supposed to touch one of the moving dots as the birds flew around on the screen. When he started playing, he couldn't even see the birds, much less the dots!

Between working out with Rick and playing games on his computer, John stayed busy. Plus, when friends told him he should write a book about his miraculous recovery from the motorcycle accident, he thought *Why not?* Patti Kohrt, a longtime family friend who had recently been hired on at Star Operators, offered to compile and organize the information and stories. Margie Knight, a freelance writer, agreed to serve as John's ghostwriter and co-author. They titled the book *A Miracle on the Road to Recovery.* The collection of stories and memories was released in March of 2010. Patti's husband created a website— Johnkellersmiracle.com—telling John's story, featuring videos and offering hope to families of traumatic brain injury victims.

And while John's recovery *had* been a miracle, since waking up he had been terrified of one thing: getting stuck. And now the very thing he had feared appeared to be happening. His body was healing—his stamina, balance and even bladder control had returned—but his brain was still broken.

He still talked too loud and said too much. He had a ten-minute memory. He couldn't multitask. He lost his cell phone consistently throughout the day. Lacking social filters, he interrupted people, saying anything that came to mind. He had angry outbursts and felt anxious. He dominated every conversation to hide the fact that he couldn't mentally track with the discussion. He still cornered strangers and told them every detail of his accident. And he was still passive and insecure as a dad.

> She turned back to James. "If we don't do something, John could spend the rest of his life as a four-year-old trapped in an adult's body."

John's family had hoped that the Lumosity® games might help him close the gap between where he was and where he needed to be. But after months of playing the digital brain training games, John was losing interest. He had passed all the levels, so the games were no longer challenging.

They also weren't translating into real-life changes. While John was getting faster at winning the games, his new skills weren't changing the way his brain performed in day-to-day situations—except for his eyes. After spending countless hours trying to touch the dots on the backs of those flying birds, John had improved at visually following objects in real life.

But when it came to the better memory, faster processing and sharper logic & reasoning John desperately needed to reclaim his life, nothing had changed at all.

One Sunday morning at Jennifer's church, the pastor showed the congregation a short video about John and asked them to pray for his progress. A few weeks later, a friend of Jennifer's stopped her after church and asked how John was doing. Then she told Jennifer that her daughter had completed a brain training program with a trainer from LearningRx.

"We can't believe the difference it's made," she said. "Brittney isn't frustrated all the time anymore. She can pay attention and remember things like never before. Even her teachers are amazed. They're saying she's a completely different kid!"

The woman added, "I didn't think you'd mind, so I played John's video for the director of the brain training center that helped Brittney so much. She told me they have programs that can help John rebuild broken connections in his brain."

Since she was a little girl, Jennifer loved church and felt she got a lot out of the experience; things like encouragement, direction and hope. On that Sunday, she walked away with all those things—plus the business card of Gina Cruz, the director of the LearningRx Brain Training Center in San Antonio, Texas. It had been a very good day.

*   *   *

After meeting with Gina, the Kellers knew they had some important decisions to make. On the four-hour drive from San Antonio back to McAllen, they talked about options.

"I don't think we have a choice." Jan lowered her voice, then relaxed when she looked over her shoulder and saw that John, in the backseat, was absorbed with a game on his phone and oblivious to their conversation.

She turned back to James. "If we don't do something, John could spend the rest of his life as a four-year-old trapped in an adult's body."

The couple agreed that John desperately needed what LearningRx could do for him. The problem was the logistics.

"Four hours," James shook his head. "That's not something you can drive every day. And moving half the family to San Antonio doesn't seem reasonable either."

"Dear Jesus," Jan said aloud, "help us know what to do."

They drove in silence for several miles.

Suddenly James hit his palm on the steering wheel. "Patti Kohrt! I can't believe I didn't think of her sooner! Once a week she could drive John to San Antonio to work with the LearningRx trainer there. The other days she could train John in McAllen. She's organized, she's smart, and she's tough enough that she'll push John, even when he stands up to her!"

Patti was, indeed, the perfect fit. She had already earned John's trust while working with him compiling stories for his book. Best of all, it would be simple for Patti to meet every day with John because she already worked at Star Operators.

The next day, James and Jan met with Patti.

James spoke first. "Patti, when you came on board a couple months ago, I knew you were overqualified for the job we were giving you to do. But I've always believed in hiring good people when I find them, even if it means finding—or creating—the right position for them later. And Patti, we found it. I think it's quite possible that God brought you here for a reason none of us suspected at the time."

"I'm listening," Patti said.

"We want to put John into a one-on-one brain training program with a company called LearningRx. We're convinced they can help him get unstuck. They improve mental skills about thirty percentile points and raise IQ fifteen to twenty points. They say they can help John's memory, vision, anxiety, listening skills—even help him remember where he left his cell phone!"

> "We want to hire one of LearningRx's brain training coaches instead of giving John more digital brain training for the same reason we hired Rick instead of handing John a workout video."

Patti knitted her brows in thought. "Hasn't he been doing brain training? On the computer?"

James shrugged. "That's what we thought, but they're actually very different things."

Jan added, "We asked Gina about it. We needed to know because, as you can imagine, if her programs were the same thing we'd already been doing, there'd be no point."

"What's the difference?" Patti asked.

"Digital brain training is great for keeping a healthy brain healthy, but it's not really designed to create the kind of big, life changing improvements John needs," James said. "It's like ordering a workout DVD and telling yourself you'll work out in front of your TV when you want to—versus hiring a drill sergeant who shows up every day, gets you out of your comfort zone, and pushes you farther than you thought you could go."

Jan added, "We want to hire one of LearningRx's brain training coaches instead of giving John more digital brain training for the same reason we hired Rick instead of handing John a workout video."

"That's where you come in," James said. "We need someone who will drive John up to San Antonio every week, at least to start. But we also need someone smart and tough—"

"And compassionate," Jan added

"And compassionate—who will work with John for an hour or two a day here in McAllen, five days a week. The person needs to be a combination teacher, coach, and drill sergeant."

Patti laughed. "Drill sergeant? What are you saying?"

The Kellers had been friends with Patti and her family for years. James smiled. "Look—you're able to keep your husband in line."

"Touché," she nodded good-naturedly. "OK, you've got a deal."

6

A Leap of Faith

The Boeing 192 lifted off the runway and Gina felt herself pressed backward into her seat as the jet began to climb.

It was the week after her consultation with the Keller family. She'd chatted with them by phone the day before and agreed with James and Jan that having Patti do some of John's training in McAllen was a great idea. In a couple weeks, Patti and John would drive to San Antonio. John would have his first session with Catherine, a LearningRx certified brain trainer, then Catherine would teach Patti how to become John's brain training coach at home.

Today, however, Gina was winging her way from Texas to Colorado for the annual three-day LearningRx convention. Owners, directors and staff from every LearningRx Center across the country would be attending. There would be workshops and roundtables. One of the guest speakers was a renowned researcher conducting a study on how LearningRx brain training physically changes the brain—and he had functional magnetic resonance imaging (fMRI) brain scans to prove it! Gina couldn't wait to hear what he had to say.

Gina's mom, Kathy DeLeon, worked with Gina at the San Antonio Northeast Center and was accompanying her to the convention. Gina's husband and business partner, Gabriel, was back home in San Antonio, holding down the fort with Gabriel Jr., fourteen, and Elijah, five.

Thinking of her boys, Gina couldn't help but smile.

Truth be told, she probably wouldn't be in the brain training business at all if it wasn't for her first son, Gabriel Jr., who was born with special needs.

Shortly after Gabriel Jr. was born, Gina got a job as a special education teacher. She loved helping kids and their families, but wasn't crazy about the limitations imposed by the public school system. In fact, the longer she worked in special education, the more she could see that making modifications and accommodations for students with special needs wasn't the answer. It was a temporary fix, a band-aid, a crutch. She longed to offer kids and their families a permanent solution that would actually *fix* the problem, and having her own child with special needs just made Gina all the more passionate about finding solutions.

The first time she heard about LearningRx, she realized it was different than any other program out there. The company specialized in taking the latest in brain science and applying it to help kids and adults get faster, smarter brains.

They did this by pairing their clients with personal trainers who worked with them one-on-one, an hour a day, for roughly twelve to thirty-two weeks.

The LearningRx brain training coaching system was not only research-based and clinically proven, it provided real-life solutions for *anyone* wanting to think faster and better. Their clients included struggling students, high-achieving students, senior adults, adults wanting to excel in their careers, and individuals with dyslexia, ADHD, autism or even traumatic brain injuries.

In fact, the doctor who pioneered this approach and founded the company had suffered from dyslexia himself when he was a boy. No wonder he had such a passion for struggling kids!

And the coaching really worked. The improvements clients were making in how their brains worked were unmatched by anything Gina had seen in her career in education. One-on-one brain training was even clinically proven to increase IQ.

It was a leap of faith, really. Gina and Gabriel didn't have the money to purchase a franchise, and the day Gina flew to the LearningRx headquarters in Colorado Springs to sign the papers and pay the franchise fees, the bank hadn't even approved her loan yet.

It was approved in the nick of time.

There were actually lots of moments like that. Gina calls them her miracles. As she later explained to a friend, "Through the whole process of starting this business, I kept praying for God either to open the doors wide so I could go forward, or slam them shut if this was a path he didn't want me to take. And the doors just kept opening.

"I try to live by faith, and by Jeremiah 29:11. That's the verse where God says, 'For I know the plans I have for you. They are plans for good and not for disaster, to give you a future and a hope.' Starting this business isn't just about a future and a hope for me and my family. It's also about giving a future and a hope to every kid and grownup who walks through those front doors."

One of those kids was a fifth grader named Chelsea.

When Chelsea first came to LearningRx, the ten-year-old was struggling in school, with friendships, and with anxiety so severe that she felt compelled to pull her hair out.

Through testing, Gina was able to discover the root cause of Chelsea's struggles: She was well below the fiftieth percentile in nearly half of her cognitive skills. No wonder she was struggling and stressed!

After working with her LearningRx brain training coach, Chelsea's improvements were dramatic:

Her logic and reasoning improved the most, from the thirty-eighth percentile to the seventy-seventh. And in

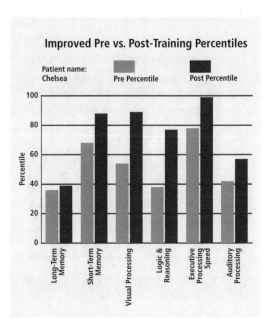

Improved Pre vs. Post-Training Percentiles

Patient name: Chelsea   Pre Percentile   Post Percentile

Percentile (y-axis: 0, 20, 40, 60, 80, 100)

Categories: Long-Term Memory, Short-Term Memory, Visual Processing, Logic & Reasoning, Executive Processing Speed, Auditory Processing executive processing, she jumped from the seventy-eighth to the ninety-ninth percentile! Finally, three of Chelsea's skills—short-term memory, visual processing and executive processing speed—improved so much they exceeded the eighty-first percentile, which is the average score of college-bound students.

Chelsea's faster, smarter brain made learning easier, and her grades improved.

But the improvement that most endeared Chelsea to Gina had to do with Chelsea's hair: It was beautiful! Now that Chelsea wasn't so stressed and anxious, she had stopped pulling it out! Chelsea isn't shy anymore, either. In fact, the girl who couldn't make a friend has lots of friends now.

For this little girl, one-on-one brain training was absolutely life changing.

Another client Gina would never forget was Marcos. When the eleven-year-old walked into the San Antonio LearningRx Center, he was on ADHD medication. He had a hard time remembering directions and staying on-task at school and at home. At school, his grades were suffering. At home, there was often tension with family members. And while the medication was helping, there were side effects—like not sleeping at night—that neither Marcos nor his parents felt good about.

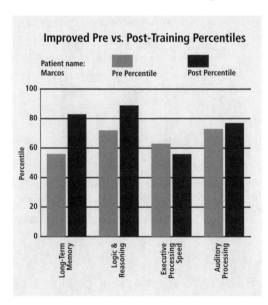

Before his twelve-week brain training program was finished, Marcos had improved so much, his doctor took him completely off all ADHD medication. Marcos was also doing better in school, plus homework was taking half the time, relieving tensions at home. Best of all, Marcos was beginning to see himself in a whole new light. He wasn't "the kid who struggled" anymore. He was actually turning into someone excited about what his future held, at school and beyond!

But one of Gina's most memorable clients so far had to be "the bawling woman."

Gina hadn't been open for business too long—perhaps a few months—when she found herself sitting in her office listening to someone crying in a training room down the hall.

Actually, Beatrice was bawling.

The forty-two-year-old woman had struggled her whole life with poor memory, slow thinking and low self-esteem. In her first meeting with Gina, she confessed that she had been ashamed to even walk into the LearningRx Center because she thought she was too old. She was convinced it was too late to improve her life. As she explained to Gina, her grown children were all smarter than she was, and she was so very tired of always feeling like the least intelligent person in the room.

And now, just two weeks into brain training, the woman was positively sobbing.

Gina put down her pencil, sat back in her chair and listened in awe to the sound of Beatrice weeping for joy.

Gina knew Beatrice was weeping for joy because, between sobs, she kept shouting, "I couldn't do this a week ago! Now I can do this! This is helping me so much…I'm so glad I'm here…I'm so very glad I came in…I can't believe I can do this! I'm really doing this!!"

Gina thought, *Wow! This is why I'm here: to help this person change her life. It's the reason I stepped out in faith and started this business. This woman's entire world is in the process of being transformed, and I get to be a part of this! Wow!*

The seat belt light in the console above Gina's head began to blink and a flight attendant, speaking over the loudspeaker, launched into the customary instructions about preparing for landing.

Gina gazed out the window at the rapidly approaching tarmac. In a matter of weeks, John Keller would begin a fascinating new leg of his miraculous journey out of the twilight he'd been living in. She knew the Keller family was excited and hopeful, but also a little nervous and unsure of what to expect.

In the six years she'd owned the San Antonio Center, Gina had helped more than five hundred kids and adults succeed in their quest to enjoy a better life by improving the way they thought, reasoned, read, learned, remembered and even paid attention.

She knew very well what lay ahead.

Gina was absolutely certain that she and her team could get John Keller unstuck and making the progress he so desperately needed to make.

7
Mental Sweat

After working at the San Antonio Northeast Brain Training Center for almost three years, Catherine Lee had established herself as the center's most effective trainer. Now, as assistant director, she spent most of her time training the other trainers who worked in the office. When she did take on a client, it was usually one of the more challenging cases.

She had recently worked with another TBI patient, a man in his forties. His improvements were astonishing. Granted, his injury wasn't as severe as John's, but the changes Catherine had witnessed left her more convinced than ever that teaming up with a brain training coach can be absolutely life changing for people with TBIs.

Her confidence in the program was a good thing, since she suspected John Keller was about to pose the greatest challenge of any client she'd ever worked with.

Their first training session together proved her right.

Leading John to a training room, Catherine gestured him into a chair facing her's across a table. Before Catherine could say a word, John rushed headlong into a confusing monologue about his accident. She could tell that John didn't know what he remembered and what he didn't, though he tried to cover up that fact by being funny. He was turned around in every area of life. And the whole time, he was talking, talking, talking…

At one point he said, "I flew across the cars like this," and started throwing pencils.

Catherine had tested and trained a lot of people with TBIs, and many of them didn't have a filter and consequently said whatever came to mind. But John's excessive talking, and not being able to control speed or volume—well, she'd never seen *that* before.

John went into that first brain training session with the goal of hiding his identity as Captain Caveman. He'd privately given himself that nickname because, with little memory and limited vision, that's how he felt—primitive and isolated—which he found both frustrating and embarrassing.

> John hoped all the caffeine was speeding up his brain. He didn't realize it was just making him jittery, giving him insomnia and sending him crashing into an energy slump by mid-afternoon.

He often scolded himself with the thought, *I gotta get outta this cave!* But it was hard to have the energy to overcome his struggles when he was expending so much energy trying to cover them up.

One of the ways he tried to cover-up was by monopolizing every conversation.

Another strategy was to drink coffee. Lots of coffee. As in ten-cups-a-day. He hoped all the caffeine was speeding up his brain and masking his memory loss. He didn't realize it was simply making him jittery, giving him insomnia, and sending him crashing into an energy slump by mid-afternoon.

After getting John's attention away from telling his story and onto their training session, Catherine gave him a preview of what to expect over the coming weeks and months. When she handed him his LearningRx backpack, she definitely saw interest flash across his face. The backpack contained a collection of intriguing tools: a workbook, metronome, stopwatch and various puzzles, cards and games.

These tools were for training, not teaching. They were, in fact, the mental barbells, dumbbells, jump ropes, leg presses and chin-up bars that John and Catherine would use together to strengthen his brain. The workbook contained literally hundreds of levels which would allow

Catherine to target John's weaknesses, customize his workouts and push him hardest in the areas in which he needed the most change.

The purpose of each exercise was actually different than what it seemed. For example, when Catherine asked John to add numbers in his head and solve a puzzle at the same time, she wouldn't be doing it to teach him new math or puzzle skills. Instead, she would be using that particular combination of exercises to create "mental sweat"—to tax John's current mental abilities. This would, in turn, stimulate his brain to respond by firing up weak, dormant or even brand-new neural connections. In other words, changing John's brain depended less on learning the "right" answers and more on the mental grunting and sweating of wrestling with challenges that felt slightly out of reach.

To change John's brain more quickly and with permanent results, Catherine would be adding two elements: *intensity* and something called *loading*. She would do this by pushing John to perform many of the exercises in the midst of distractions, against the clock, or while juggling several tasks at once.

As a result, John *would* improve at math and puzzles—but not because he'd learned something new. He would improve at math and puzzles (and not just math and puzzles, but anything else he set out to do or learn) because from that point forward for the rest of his life he would be working with stronger cognitive skills and a faster, smarter brain.

From their very first session, Catherine could see that simply keeping John contained for an hour would be a challenge. He was always asking to eat, or blow his nose, or use the bathroom. Catherine had never seen anyone use so many excuses to avoid answering a question or doing a task.

Several times during their first session, John got downright argumentative.

While memorizing a list of words, he said hotly, "Why do I need to do this? This is stupid!"

"What if you want to go to the grocery store? How will you remember your list?"

"I put it in my cell phone. I put everything in my cell phone. It's why I don't need this program. I'm fine. I don't need a better memory."

There he was—Captain Caveman—desperate to stay incognito.

Catherine leaned back in her chair, her head cocked to one side, and studied John. "OK, so where's your cell phone now?"

"What?"

"Do you know where your phone is right now?"

John thought a moment. He thought some more. His shoulders dropped a little.

Finally he admitted, "I can't remember."

The next day, John met with Patti at the Star Operators office for more brain training. Catherine had showed Patti exactly what to do, so she was ready.

Patti placed a sheet of paper face down on the desk between them.

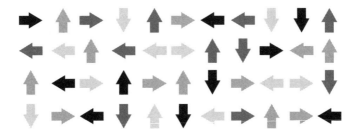

Hidden from John's view for the moment, the paper consisted of row after row of arrows. Each arrow was a different color—blue, black, red, orange or green—and each pointed a different direction: up, down, right or left.

"John, when I say go, I want you to turn the paper over and tell me the color of each arrow in the first three rows."

"Got it!" John exclaimed.

Patti looked at her watch. "You have two minutes. Ready...and... Go!"

"Red. Red. Blue. Black. Orange..." John completed the exercise in about a minute.

Patti put a metronome on the table and told John to do it again, this time naming the colors on beat. In future sessions, Patti would crank up the intensity with distractions, multitasking and challenging twists, like alternating naming the color with naming the direction of the arrow. But for this first session, she and John had accomplished what they'd set out to do. After several more repetitions, John was able to cut his time in less than half. What had taken him a minute to do, he was now able to do in twenty-five seconds.

To John, this meant a lot more than simply picking up speed. It was a gift of hope and confidence. After all, if his brain could do this, what else could it do? He felt the specter of Captain Caveman recede ever so slightly into the shadows.

Just as Jan and April played crucial roles in John's eleven-month journey from the accident to waking up, Catherine and Patti were key players in John's journey to rebuild vital connections in his brain.

From the first time they met, Catherine could see that Patti was strong in spirit and detail-minded. Catherine couldn't have been more pleased. It was going to be a very good partnership.

Patti kept track of everything she did with John. Every day she logged his exercises, results, time spent completing each exercise, his complaints, even his bathroom breaks. Then she e-mailed the information to Catherine. Her attention to detail enabled Catherine to monitor John's progress closely from afar.

Patti was also able to work well with John. She was always pleasant, but she could hold her ground too. When John complained about an exercise, she would say nicely but firmly, "It doesn't matter if you like it or not. You're going to do it anyway."

One of the first improvements everyone noticed was that John was becoming more self-aware. Within two weeks, he could tell when he was talking too loud and lower his voice without someone prompting him.

Shortly after that, John walked into Catherine's office and asked, "Can you tell that I'm walking straighter?" Later that same morning he asked, "Can you tell that my voice is more calm?"

Other days John would ask Catherine if she could see that his eyes were less dilated, or that he could sit still longer without having to get up.

Before brain training, John wasn't even aware that these things needed to be changed!

John was also starting to remember where he left things. As his visual processing skills got stronger, he learned how to take a snapshot in his mind of where he put his cell phone, keys and other items. His eyes, which had quivered left and right since the accident, were also beginning to settle down.

At home one day, John thrilled his mom when, out of the blue, he turned to her and said, "Guess what? I know where my keys are." Another day he came to breakfast and told Jan, "I was looking everywhere for this shirt," pointing to the shirt he was wearing, "when I remembered where I had put it in my closet."

And with more confidence, John found he needed less caffeine. He started drinking less coffee, which made him a lot calmer and less jittery.

What James noticed the most was John's shift from monologue to dialogue. For over a year John had talked only about himself: the accident, how he'd been working out and his arms were getting bigger, and so on. Suddenly he was asking questions, listening and following other people's comments and thoughts.

One day Catherine mentioned, "The next time you come to San Antonio for training, it'll be my birthday." When John returned two weeks later, he brought her a birthday present of a plate of cookies.

Two more weeks passed before John had another training session in San Antonio. When he arrived, Catherine asked him, "What did you do different the last time we were together?"

"I brought you a present," he answered, with a big smile on his face.

"And what did you bring me?

"Chocolate chip cookies!"

As far as Catherine was concerned, sweeter words had never been spoken.

8

Transitions

About that time, John hit a wall. He began showing up late for his training sessions and was unable to focus. He grew increasingly lackadaisical, irritable and belligerent, which were then reflected in his progress.

One day when John arrived over an hour late for training, Patti took a stand. Intercepting John at the doorway to his office, she said calmly, "You know what, John? If you're not interested in doing this, I have better things to do with my time." Then she turned and walked back to her desk.

After ten minutes or so, he followed her there. "OK, I'm ready to work now."

"Not today," she said without even glancing up from her computer. "I have other things to do now. I rearranged my schedule this morning to work with you, and you weren't interested. We'll try again tomorrow."

A few days later she asked John point blank what was going on.

"It's me and April," he admitted. "We're fighting a lot."

Patti softened. In fact, John was so distraught and distracted that Patti—the drill sergeant!—cancelled brain training for a few days.

John's traumatic brain injury had turned his and April's world upside down. The plot—and even the characters—of their lives had changed dramatically. They were going to counseling. They were trying hard to make their marriage work.

They just weren't having any success.

The truth was that, for John and April both, it was becoming harder to deny that the accident may have totaled something far more precious than John's motorcycle.

When the mayor's office in McAllen caught wind of John's TBI and miraculous progress, John was invited to speak for fifteen minutes at the city's annual prayer luncheon. Before the event, John focused on his gym workouts, brain training, and upcoming speaking engagement.

With help from his dad, John prepared by scribbling his notes onto index cards. Instead of writing full sentences or shorthand notes, he wrote the first letter of every word in each sentence. "Thank you for inviting me to this prayer breakfast" turned into "Tyfimttpb." Card after card contained a seemingly indecipherable mess of letters only John could understand.

This method had worked for him before his brain injury. He hoped it would work for him now, too.

The day of the prayer luncheon, the master of ceremonies introduced John by showing a video of him in a wheelchair at TIRR. Following the video, the emcee called John to the podium. As John jumped to his feet and walked to the stage, the crowd of four hundred erupted in wild applause, blown away by the contrast between the video image they had just seen of John in the wheelchair and the vivacious, grinning man standing behind the lectern.

With an uncommon degree of composure, John waited for the applause to wane before he began speaking. John's dad sitting on the platform, and his mom in the audience, later said they felt more nervous than John looked! Before the accident, John hated speaking in public. But on that day he was in his element. He felt completely at home. Not even having to stoop his six feet, five inch frame to reach a short microphone seemed to rattle him.

John began to speak. For the next fifteen minutes, he had the audience laughing and crying—sometimes at the same time!

During his address he thanked the mayor for the invitation, and the emergency response team and the McAllen Medical Center staff for saving his life. But he mostly talked about the power of prayer.

"I am a living testimony of the power of prayer, and what the Devil wanted back, God made better, and what was going to be a tragedy, God turned into triumph."

As he finished, the crowd gave him a standing ovation. The mayor awarded John with a key to the city. Everyone burst into applause a second time.

KELLER HOME VIDEO
"Prayer Luncheon"
Scan with smartphone or visit
vitalconnectionsbook.com

Walking out of the McAllen Convention Center that day, John felt like he was on top of the world.

*   *   *

The brain training system that was changing John's life wasn't a fad. In fact, the whole thing began forty years earlier with the simple question, "How can we help people learn easier and faster?"

It was the early '70s, and the question was being asked by Dr. Ken Gibson, a pediatric optometrist and specialist in visual processing.

Determined to find the answer, Dr. Gibson began compiling clinical experiences with children and adults. In addition to his own practice, he founded preschools and learning centers and worked with kids in those settings, too.

He also began researching the latest developments in any field or science related to the brain, and applying those developments to his growing body of work.

Soon he discovered an interesting pattern. He realized that students were paying attention better and recalling important facts more easily after being coached through short but intense periods of mental exercise. The doctor was intrigued. Could these results be replicated? Could a program of intense mental exercise, done one-on-one in a coaching environment, improve brain performance to the point that learning would come easier? Deciding to test his theory on thirty-five students who were struggling in school, Gibson created a three-month program. Unlike any learning remedy that had been attempted before, the program wasn't based on tutoring or classroom instruction; instead, it consisted of mental workouts designed to strengthen the brain. Could it change the way these students performed in school?

The results were far better than the good doctor had dared hope.

After just three months, these students jumped ahead in their learning skills and performance by nearly three years! Ken Gibson was on to something. He was truly changing the brain in ways that made learning and thinking easier than before.

As the news of his findings spread, doctors, psychologists, teachers and other professionals began asking to use the Gibson method with their own patients. Soon, more than two thousand professionals had been trained and were using these techniques. More importantly, the program continued getting unprecedented results. Improvements that had once taken eighteen months to achieve through tutoring and other therapies were being accomplished in just three months by doing the innovative Gibson procedures with a brain training coach.

The intense mental workouts were proving to be life changing for kids with learning problems. Could they help kids with greater challenges, including more severe learning disabilities, dyslexia or autism?

Dr. Gibson continued taking the latest developments in brain research and using them to help kids improve how they thought, learned, read, remembered and even paid attention. Soon students with ADHD, dyslexia, memory deficits and other learning disabilities were getting dramatic improvements, too.

In 2002, an entrepreneur went through the program with his son. Thrilled with the results, he and a business partner persuaded Ken to open a local center so families could have access to the Gibson brain training methods and coaches.

The next year, seven more centers opened. Ken called the company LearningRx.

In the meantime, the number of people benefiting from Dr. Gibson's brain training methods was also expanding. Soon, career adults, good students wanting to excel, kids and adults with autism, senior adults wanting to avoid dementia, victims of strokes and people with traumatic brain injuries were finding the solutions they needed at LearningRx.

More than forty years of clinical research had gone into the coaching program on which the Keller family had hung their hopes. And apparently they'd made the right choice, because it was definitely working.

*　　　*　　　*

One night John reviewed a sales spreadsheet for his dad. John was tired, and he had to strain to see the tiny numbers, and the project took a very, very long time. But he didn't give up. He pushed through, knowing the next time he tried something like this it would be easier, and the time after that easier still.

If his brain training coach had taught him anything, it was how to push through challenges that felt just a little beyond reach.

One of the biggest challenges John faced was making sure he rebuilt strong connections with his sons. Whenever Caden and Dalton came to visit, John took over making most of their meals, even if it was as simple as assembling peanut butter sandwiches or nuking corn dogs. And with his improved memory, he became a more confident parent. He didn't let the boys get away with as much. He took them swimming. He taught them how to help him wash his truck.

Learning how to be a good dad was more important to John than ever. John's brain injury had cost him his marriage. He was determined not to let it rob him of being a dad to Caden and Dalton.

On his next visit to San Antonio, John was sitting across the training table with Catherine when, halfway through their session, he suddenly grinned.

"What's so funny?" Catherine asked.

"Hey. Ask me where my cell phone is."

"OK, where's your cell phone?"

"It's lying face down in the cup holder in the front seat of the car."

To a casual observer, the exchange would hold little meaning. To Catherine and anyone else who'd played a role in John's miraculous journey—and especially to John himself—it was a symbol of a brand new life.

9
Pebbles in the Pond

Even the smallest pebble pelting the surface of a pond sends concentric circles rippling outward, stirring everything in its path.

Imagine the ripple effect of a thirty-six-hundred-pound Chevy Lumina!

Countless lives had been impacted by John's accident, including the unsuspecting family in the car, first responders, surgeons, nurses, physical therapists, family, friends, employees and more.

A marriage had ended.

Life had changed forever for Caden and Dalton.

Jené's and Jennifer's blog about John's recovery had been read by thousands of people—many who knew John and others who didn't—and had attracted more than one hundred thousand visits.

People had rallied to pray. Many folks say that, in watching John's recovery, they witnessed a true miracle.

Even John's personality had spun in an entirely new trajectory. In the American folktale, the likeable Rip Van Winkle falls asleep for years and awakens to a very different world, in which he is reunited with his now-grown children. In John's case, however, a brilliant workaholic fell asleep for a year, waking to discover he'd been changed into a child. Eventually he was transformed, not back into his type-A personality, but into a gregarious, youthful adult. Talk about changes!

John's motorcycle accident had created a lot more than ripples; it had created waves, impacting everyone within reach—sometimes bearing gifts, sometimes bringing tragedy.

And there were still more changes to come.

The Kellers had already been leading a quarterly support workshop during which families impacted by traumatic brain injuries were given a chance to share their stories and talk about solutions to common challenges. One day a TIRR chaplain invited them to participate in a volunteer program that would allow them to reach an even greater number of TBI patients and their families.

As part of this program, James, Jan and John would be allowed to walk the halls of TIRR, going into hospital rooms of TBI patients to encourage—and pray with—these patients and their families. Of course, in order to do this, they would have to drive six hours from McAllen to Houston—and six hours back again! But it was an opportunity to offer desperately needed support and answers to hurting families, so the Kellers gladly accepted the invitation!

Every time that John, James and Jan made the trip to TIRR, the chaplain gave them a list of patients who could benefit from their particular brand of sunshine. Before long the family was driving to Houston every six weeks or so.

During one trip, they met a young man who was so depressed and discouraged, he spoke of giving up.

"You can't quit," John urged. "Sure, you're going to feel depressed some days—that's part of the brain injury. But you can't let it take over your life. If you refuse to give up, if you do everything your therapists tell you to do, your life will get better."

Later the man's wife texted John, "I don't know what my husband would have done without your encouragement!"

John, once too busy for people, began walking up to complete strangers—often in wheelchairs and sometimes missing parts of their skulls—and saying without trepidation, "Can I pray for you?"

The Kellers met with a gunshot victim, businessmen with brain damage as a result of heart attacks, teenagers who had hit their heads while playing school sports, men and women who had survived auto accidents and more.

Sometimes they arrived armed with photos of John when he was at his worst. James and Jan would tell the families of patients, "Look, John was much worse than your loved one. But see where he is now? There's hope for your family member, too."

James and Jan had been involved as leaders in church youth ministry for nearly forty years. Because of that, they knew lots of men and women, now adults, who had once been under their leadership. Such was the case with Mark. He'd once been a teenager in the Keller's youth group. Now he was fifty-one and had suffered a massive heart attack on a golf course. By the time paramedics could get his heart going again, his brain had gone too long without oxygen. Doctors had no good news for the family.

Beyond discouraged and approaching despair, Mark's parents welcomed the visit from their son's former youth pastors. When Jan encouraged Mark's mom to keep praying, reminding her that prayer makes a difference, the distraught mother shook her head. "What if it's God's will for Mark to stay like this?" she asked.

"God's will is to bless your family," Jan said, "You *have* to pray and believe. And if nothing happens, all I can say is that—this side of heaven—we may not get all the answers we're seeking, but at least we'll know we tried."

Looking at Mark, Jan added, "I see the same look in his eyes that I saw in John's. He's frustrated that he can't move. That's a good sign. Keep praying. Don't give up."

A month later, Mark's family found themselves in the same situation the Kellers had faced, with their insurance company making the decision to release Mark from TIRR unless he could show further progress. Mark's doctor looked him in the eye and said, "Mark, if you do something for me today, we can keep you here. But you have to show me what you can do."

Mark walked 141 steps that day.

His mother texted Jan two simple but miraculous words: "He's walking!"

Time and time again, the Kellers delivered their message of hope to hurting families: *We know you're getting bad news. We know you're being told there's no hope. But don't believe it. The brain is not only an amazing organ that can fire neurons in new paths around damaged areas, but prayer works, and God does miracles. And that's why you can't always go by what you see. Keep believing and never give up.*

As the story of John's dramatic recovery began to spread, a Houston television station aired a story about him.

National Public Radio (NPR) interviewed him for a story on Congresswoman Gabrielle Giffords following the tragic shooting that left her with a much-publicized traumatic brain injury.

Chicken Soup for the Soul® featured John's story as a chapter in the book *Boost Your Brain Power*.

KELLER HOME VIDEO
"Student of the Year"
Scan with smartphone or visit
vitalconnectionsbook.com

In addition, LearningRx recognized John as the 2011 Student of the Year and featured him in their very own *Life Changing Magazine*.

In the meantime, John continued getting invitations to speak. One day he shared his story with a Fellowship of Christian Athletes chapter. After the meeting, some of the young men challenged him to a competition to see who could do the most push-ups. John more than kept up with his competitors. Most of the teenage athletes dropped out, but John never quit—in fact, he did so many push-ups that he lost count of the number. When John finished, his shirt was soaked through with sweat, but he felt exhilarated to be alive.

Life, John realized, was good. And one of the reasons it was so satisfying was because he was able to encourage others out of the pain, challenges, losses and victories that he and his family had experienced.

One day John walked into the room of a brain-injured patient at TIRR. The forty-something-year-old man laying in bed didn't respond much, but the woman sitting in the chair beside his bed began to cry.

"This is my husband," she said through tears, gesturing toward the man in the bed. "We have two small children. When I was researching where to take my husband, I saw a link to a video about you on TIRR's website. Watching that video made the difference. It's why we came here. I never would have thought we'd get to meet you, and here you are walking into our room!"

On another day, the Kellers met a beautiful family whose teenage daughter had tried to commit suicide. Amber didn't die, but she lost oxygen for long enough that her brain was severely damaged. Doctors said she would be a vegetable for the rest of her life; that she would never walk or talk again.

The first thing the Kellers noticed was that, while Amber wasn't talking, she wasn't exactly lifeless. In fact, the teenager was laying on her back in bed, thrashing about with her feet in the air. It looked like she was pedaling.

After watching Amber for a moment, Jan said matter-of-factly, "She's a track runner."

Amber's mother looked surprised. "How did you know?"

"That's what she's doing. She's running."

"Doctors say it's just reflexes."

"No, she wants out of here," Jan observed. "I want your family to encourage her. Cheer her on. I want you to yell, 'Go, Amber!'"

Soon Amber was walking and talking. Jan told the family it looked like Amber would soon be ready for the next phase of her recovery: one-on-one brain training at LearningRx!

The Kellers are adamant that, based on what LearningRx brain training has done for John, it can help anyone.

"It gave him his life back," Jan says.

John continues making improvements with LearningRx brain training. But tests already confirm that changes in John's brain have transformed how he is able to function in every area of his life. John's long-term memory has improved by leaps and bounds, jumping from the first percentile to the fifty-first. His visual and auditory processing skills show even greater improvement. Logic and reasoning are up by forty percentile points, from the nineteenth to the fifty-ninth percentiles. Finally, his processing speed and executive processing speed show tremendous improvements as well. Even more importantly, the changes in John's brain are permanent.

And the circles continue to ripple outward.

Recently, six-year-old Caden started working with his own LearningRx brain training coach. LearningRx has a program called

LiftOff® specifically designed for preschool, kindergarten and first grade students. It helps prepare their brains for school, and gives them a powerful jump-start to successful reading and spelling. John says the program has been like "turning on a light switch" for his son, adding, "Caden's confidence and focus have increased dramatically—just like mine!"

Once a week Rick Vasquez, accompanied by John, drives Caden to San Antonio to meet with his brain training coach.

John loves encouraging his son. He often says, "Caden, after brain training you'll be able to do so much more than you can do now! Look how smart you are already! You're a genius!"

Recently the Keller family went on vacation. John sat in the backseat of their Suburban with Dalton, Caden and one of Caden's friends. They were talking and laughing when suddenly Caden looked up at his dad and said, "Daddy, I think you don't have a brain injury anymore!"

Without a doubt, life for this family is different than it was before the accident, and there are still improvements to make. In many ways, healing will be a lifelong process.

But John Keller, the man and the dad, is back.

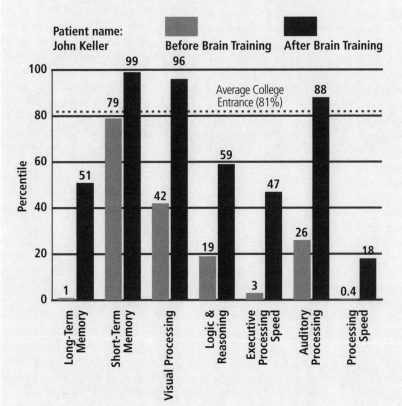

Cognitive Skills Profile:
Improved Post-Training Percentiles

Percentile scores represent where an individual ranks out of 100

Patient name: John Keller

Before Brain Training

After Brain Training

Percentile

100

80

60

40

20

0

Average College Entrance (81%)

99
96
79
51
42
19
59
3
47
26
88
0.4
18
1

Long-Term Memory

Short-Term Memory

Visual Processing

Logic & Reasoning

Executive Processing Speed

Auditory Processing

Processing Speed

Epilogue
Vital Connections

"I'd like to introduce you to someone whose life was changed at TIRR Memorial Hermann. John Keller, would you come up?"

The board of directors for Memorial Hermann Hospital, the largest not-for-profit healthcare system in Texas, had gathered to figure out how to raise one hundred million dollars to build a state-of-the-art brain injury wing at TIRR, their award-winning rehabilitation and research hospital.

John had been invited to speak.

Just like at the mayor's prayer luncheon, the audience seemed to expect their speaker to arrive in a wheelchair. Instead, John jumped from his seat and ran to the front of the boardroom. The men and women, dressed in formal business attire, looked surprised. He definitely had their attention.

John got right to the point.

"Three years ago, I went for a ride on my motorcycle in McAllen and wound up in Houston. I should have died, but God had other plans for me. You were part of God's plan for me too. I suffered a traumatic brain injury and spent 70 days in a coma and 344 days in the hospital—most of those days at TIRR. I drove up here from McAllen to say one thing to you today..."

John turned to the person sitting closest to him, shook his hand and said, "Thank you…"

He began working his way around the conference table.

"Thank you…Thank you…" He was shaking hands and thanking each person. When he got to the chairman of the board, the man wept.

John stopped after a dozen people and turned around. "Without you, I wouldn't be here. I'm the happiest person in this room right now, and my miracle began with you."

John's miracle is still unfolding as his brain continues to recover. His vision is greatly improved, although he still experiences some blurring in his right eye that keeps him from driving (except, of course, when Rick lets him behind the wheel for an occasional spin on an isolated road or quiet parking lot). His eyes are slightly dilated, but again, the recovery from a TBI can be slow. His sense of smell is finally returning too.

The Bible, which the Kellers look to for spiritual direction, says, "In all things God works for the good of those who love him." The Kellers believe that, while God didn't cause the accident or John's TBI, he has certainly used it in a redemptive way in John's life. On more than one occasion, James has told John, "You were such a workaholic, sometimes I think you were in a coma *before* your accident."

Every victim of a traumatic brain injury recovers differently. Factors that help determine the outcome include the severity of the injury, the area of the brain where the damage occurred and the overall ability of the body to heal.

Some of these factors are beyond the control of the average man or woman. There are other factors, however, that we can control—or at least influence—whether the trauma we're facing is to our brain, emotions, finances, career, dreams or family.

John's story paints a vivid portrait of vital connections, choices and resources that we can embrace or reject, use wisely or squander. Here's a closer look at five connections the Kellers say were instrumental in John's miraculous recovery.

Prayer

For both people of longstanding faith as well as those who have never turned to God before, prayer can indeed be a vital connection when tragedy strikes.

From the beginning, family and friends prayed for John's recovery. In fact, through his sisters' blog, thousands of people rallied to pray for John. In the distant past, the relationship between prayer and healing was discussed primarily by people in religious communities. Increasingly, however, scientific studies are recognizing a strong link between the two.

For example, studies show that people who pray tend to have lower blood pressure, less depression, lower suicide rates and stronger immune systems![1]

Prayer also makes a difference in the health and well-being of folks being prayed for. In fact, studies indicate that sick people who are prayed for by others—even if they don't know they're being prayed for—get better at a faster rate than sick people who don't have others praying for them.

In addition, a 2001 Duke University study indicated that cardiac patients who engaged in guided imagery or meditation—or who had people praying for their recovery—experienced 25 to 30 percent fewer complications following their surgeries.

While some people argue that faith is "all in your head," the Bible gives faith a lot more weight than that, going as far as to refer to faith as "substance" and "evidence": "Now faith is the substance of things hoped for, the evidence of things not seen" (Hebrews 11:1, KJV).

This verse supports the idea that the faith and prayers of John's friends and family helped shape the outcome of his experience. And indeed, James's often-repeated words to his son—"You can see better, talk better, smell better, taste better. You're better today than you were yesterday"— certainly illustrate how a father's faith helped turn something "hoped for" into reality.

Community

From the moment John's accident occurred, family rallied. Parents, stepparent, grandparents and siblings hurried to John's side. People with whom John had cultivated relationships through the years—family, best

---

[1] Cited in W. Backus, *The Healing Power of a Healthy Mind* (Minneapolis: Bethany House, 1997), 80-82.

friends, even the father of a college roommate—also began arriving to lend encouragement, prayer and support. The Keller family was also surrounded in love by the Star Operators family of employees, as well as by friendships developed through four decades of ministry.

All of these connections were vital, indeed, to this family in crisis.

It's easy to recognize the emotional support that comes from your personal communities. But researchers are discovering that the support of our friends does more than "feel good." It also has scientifically measurable benefits related to health and healing. For example, in 2006 a study of nearly three thousand nurses with breast cancer found that women who did not have close friends were four times more likely to die from the disease than women who had a thriving social network made up of ten or more friends.[2] In other studies, having a healthy number of friendships has been linked to better immune systems, fewer colds, lowered risk of heart disease and more.

Positive words and attitude

Jan asked Gina to be discreet with "bad news." She also told the nurse at TIRR that her family believed God would heal John. April declared to doctors and physical therapists that her husband would not just live, but thrive. James repeatedly told John that he was "better today than yesterday." Whether John was comatose, semicomatose or newly awake, John's family worked hard to keep their words and attitudes positive and hopeful.

The connection between maintaining a positive perspective and how our bodies respond to that perspective is scientifically proven. In fact, studies have determined that positive words can actually influence the body's recovery from injury.

Carol Ryff, a psychology professor who continues to research the link between physical and mental health, says that a positive mental attitude is more than a state of mind: "It also has linkages to what's going on in the brain and body." Ryff, and other researchers, too, say that people

[2] Candyce H. Kroenke, Laura D. Kubzansky, Eva S. Schernhammer, Michelle D. Holmes, and Ichiro Kawachi, "Social Networks, Social Support, and Survival After Breast Cancer Diagnosis," *Journal of Clinical Oncology* 24, no. 7 (March 2006), http://jco.ascopubs.org/content/24/7/1105.full.

who maintain positive thoughts and words have a lower risk of heart disease, lower levels of stress and even lower levels of inflammation.

Determination

Tommy Lasorda, famed major league baseball player and manager, has said, "The difference between the impossible and the possible lies in a person's determination."

The good news is that determination is a transferable skill. The same determination that helped us manage challenges in the past prepares us to overcome obstacles in the future. For example, John's experiences of motivating himself as an athlete and businessman served him well after he was injured, helping him push through plateaus, setbacks and obstacles encountered on the road to recovery. Even his practice of pushing his body to the limit when he was working out *before* the accident prepared him to motivate himself after the accident.

Finding a way to connect with inner resolve is imperative. A mindset that recognizes that you have overcome obstacles in the past, that you can overcome the obstacle you're facing now, and that you will continue to overcome obstacles in the future is one of your greatest assets— whether the challenge before you is related to your health, finances, career, parenting or the pursuit of a lifelong dream.

Resources

Whatever challenge you are facing—traumatic brain injury, cancer, dyslexia, ADHD and more—connecting with the right resources is key. Research your options. Know what's out there. If you're not sure where to start, look online. Read books and articles. Ask friends and family for recommendations. Find out what has worked for other people.

When John completed his insurance-funded rehabilitation, he still had a long way to go. Graduating from rehab didn't mean his recovery was complete. The Keller family continued their search for vital resources and solutions. In fact, they pursued vital resources throughout John's recovery, whether that meant locating a Level I trauma center in a larger city or finding a brain training coaching system that gets life changing results.

John's family believes strongly that, without LearningRx, John would still be an adult trying to function in life with the mental skills of a child. Jan says, "LearningRx gave John his life back."

James agrees, adding, "McAllen Medical Center and The Methodist Hospital saved John's life. TIRR woke up his brain. And LearningRx turned him from a child back into a man."

Appendices

APPENDIX A:
About LearningRx

LearningRx offers children and adults of all ages serious brain training that gets serious results:

Our clients come to us because something in their life isn't working.
Typically they are struggling at school or at work, frustrated by problems with memory, concentration, reading or the time it takes to complete tasks or assignments. Many clients have experienced concussions or TBIs, or have been diagnosed with ADHD, dyslexia or autism.

Our programs change how our clients experience life.
After going through our program, our clients experience real-life improvements in how they think, read, learn, focus and remember. They experience measurable gains at school, on the job and in daily tasks. These gains include better grades, faster completion of tasks, less procrastination, improved performance on the job, faster response times while driving or playing sports, better attention skills and improved memory.

Our results are scientifically measurable and clinically proven.
Because we do a thorough assessment of brain skills before and after brain training, we can scientifically measure the dramatic gains created by our programs. On average, our clients experience an increase of fifteen to twenty points in IQ and a gain of thirty percentile points in the seven core cognitive skills that determine how well we think, learn, read, remember and pay attention. Plus, students who come to us for help with reading typically improve their reading skills, in less than six months, an average of 2.9 years. Absolutely no other program on the market today—including tutoring or digital brain training—gets the dramatic, life changing and clinically proven results that we get.

Here's why we're so effective:

When someone comes to us for help, we begin with a comprehensive assessment of his or her cognitive skills. This helps us identify and target cognitive weaknesses that are causing problems. Then we team each client with his or her own personal brain trainer in a one-on-one coaching environment. Over the course of twelve to thirty-two weeks, clients are coached through a series of intense customized mental exercises that stimulate the brain to strengthen existing neural pathways and even forge new ones. These physical changes improve or fix weak cognitive skills, allowing the brain to work faster and more efficiently than before.

Seven things you need to know:

1. For twenty years, we've specialized in taking the latest and greatest developments in brain science and using them to help kids and adults reap the benefits of faster, smarter brains.
2. We are the pioneer and leader in the field of one-on-one brain training and the largest one-on-one brain training company in the world.
3. Our programs are researched-based and clinically proven.
4. Our results are both dramatic and scientifically measurable.
5. We help kids and adults of all ages, including struggling students, high-performing students and adults, career and senior adults. We also help kids and adults who have experienced concussions or TBIs, or who have been diagnosed with ADHD, dyslexia, autism and more.
6. One-on-one brain training is a very different process than tutoring or digital brain training, and produces radically different results.
7. We offer serious brain training that translates into significant and practical improvements in daily living.

APPENDIX B:
The Paradox of John's Memory

When John "woke up" eleven months after his accident, he had a ten-minute memory: he couldn't retain information for as long as it takes to boil an egg! At the same time, he could easily remember information—including phone numbers and passwords—learned years ago. Why could he remember things learned before his TBI but not after?

It makes sense if you know how information gets into our brains to begin with.

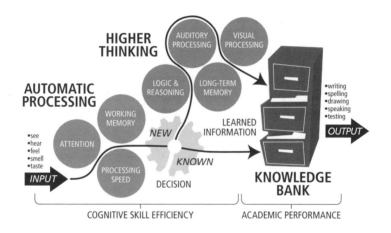

Before new information can be stored in the brain for later use, it has to be processed through a combination of underlying cognitive skills. Like cogwheels in a machine, these skills work together to move information, eventually, into stored memory. These seven skills make up IQ and determine how well we think, learn, focus and remember.

Each of our seven cognitive skills is critical. If even one is weak or damaged, it can keep the brain from grasping, remembering or using information, no matter how many times that information is presented or explained by teachers, tutors, employers, friends or family.

John's accident had damaged his brain to the point where important connections weren't being made. John's long-term memory and processing speed were practically nonexistent. His auditory and visual processing had been severely damaged, and his logic and reasoning was greatly impaired as well.

John could remember things he had learned and done before the accident because healthy cognitive skills had processed and moved those things securely into his memory bank. After the accident, however, his damaged cognitive skills simply couldn't get new information where it needed to be. Take visual processing for example. While his eyesight was improving, his world still appeared as if he were looking through the wrong end of a pair of binoculars. His peripheral vision was virtually nonexistent. He could be sitting in same room as his mom without being able to find her. He could sit at the dinner table and still be unable to find his cell phone right in front of him. Information was all around John—but his brain couldn't grasp or process what he needed to know.

To turn his life around, John needed to reroute or repair vital neural connections to get his cognitive skills up and running again.

APPENDIX C:
Results of LearningRx Pilot Program with the Washington State Department of Veterans Affairs

In January 2010, LearningRx—in partnership with the Washington State Department of Veterans Affairs and the Warrior Transition Battalion (WTB), Joint Base Lewis-McChord (JBLM) in Washington State—conducted a pilot program to train and improve the cognitive functioning of fifteen WTB active-duty service men and women who were suffering from TBIs. The training concluded in August 2010.

The program format included three hours of intensive one-on-one brain training and three hours of online brain training each week.

To measure the effectiveness of the training program, Woodcock Johnson Cognitive Abilities tests, a nationally recognized standard battery of cognitive tests, were used to conduct pre- and post-tests. WTB soldiers who entered and remained in the program gained significant improvement in all seven areas of cognitive function, including elimination of symptoms such as memory loss, poor concentration and difficulty organizing thoughts.

FORT LEWIS TBI PILOT PROGRAM USING THE LEARNINGRX ONE-ON-ONE BRAIN TRAINING SYSTEM
Percentile scores represent where an individual ranks out of 100

Cognitive Skill	Before Brain Training	After Brain Training	Percentile Gain
Processing Speed	27	76	49
Auditory Processing	26	55	29
Short-Term Memory	41	68	27
Long-Term Memory	39	65	26
Logic & Reasoning	55	75	20
Visual Processing	43	57	14
Average of All Skills	38	66	28

Testimonials

Qualitative data was also collected from the pilot program. This included the following comments:

"This impacted all areas of family, work, school and church."

"I wanted to improve my short-term memory and processing speed. They had put a big damper on my daily living by making just about everything I had to do more difficult. I have seen great improvement in these two areas. It has definitely helped."

"Thank you for being a bright light in a dark place."

"I am not in a haze. I am able to stay organized and focused."

"I definitely feel more confident in going after what I want and have enrolled in school."

"It is a great program and well worth the time invested. I would like to see it continue to be used for people with TBI."

APPENDIX D:
Compiled Results for Sixty Soldiers with TBIs Before and After LearningRx Brain Training

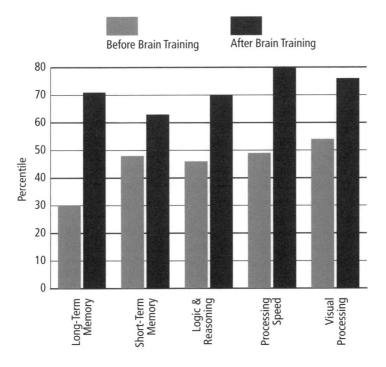

Compiled Results for Sixty Soldiers with TBIs Before and After LearningRx Brain Training

Percentile scores represent where an individual ranks out of 100

Before Brain Training   After Brain Training

(Program length, determined by severity of cognitive deficits, ranged from twelve to thirty-two weeks.)

APPENDIX E:
Real Stories. Real Families. Real Brain Training.

What if you could be smarter, think faster and remember better? In the following eight stories, you'll meet kids, teens and adults who have discovered the answer to that very question. Plus, by scanning the QR code accompanying each story with your smartphone, you can watch related videos (you can also see the videos by visiting vitalconnectionsbook.com).

"I Didn't Let Alzheimer's Steal My Future"

Maria, my brain trainer, would be arriving any minute at my apartment in the assisted living center I now called home. I wasn't completely sure what a brain trainer was, or what could be done for my failing memory, but I was about to find out!

Ever since my stroke, I had been talking slower and getting confused. I couldn't even remember my address!

But the greatest loss of all had been in the area of reading. Before my stroke, I had enjoyed reading books, magazines and my Bible every single day. Now I would read a paragraph over and over and not understand or remember anything I had read!

When a neurologist told me I was in the early stages of

BETTER MEMORY, ANYONE?

Virginia's short-term memory improved a whopping 33 percentile points! What is a percentile? If 100 students lined up according to how well they performed on a test, a student who performed as well or better than 25 percent of the other students would be 25th in line, or in the 25th percentile. After LearningRx brain training, clients with moderate to severe cognitive weaknesses "move up in line" an average of 28 percentile points. Way to go, Virginia!

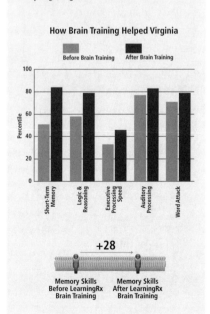

How Brain Training Helped Virginia

Alzheimer's, I was devastated. Not wanting to become a burden to my children, I sold my house, moved to an assisted living center, and waited for Alzheimer's to finish robbing me of whatever quality of life I had left.

I began to sink into depression.

That December someone gave me a book about the brain's ability to create new neurons at any age. The book mentioned a company, LearningRx, that pairs you up with a brain trainer who takes you through special mental exercises, stimulating your brain to reorganize existing neurons and even create new ones.

I got on the phone and called the LearningRx Brain Training Center in Bossier City, Louisiana, where I live. Could brain training help me? I'd soon know. There was a knock at my door. It was Maria. Before we even got started she said, "Now Virginia, I'm not giving you any shortcuts. You might be eighty-one years old, but you can do this, and I'm not cutting you any slack!"

Right away, she had me memorize the names of all the presidents of the United States by linking crazy images to each of their names.

The next time my daughter Kenda and son-in-law Randy came to visit, I rattled off the names of all forty-four presidents. Kenda said, "Mom, I couldn't even do that!"

Before long there were books and magazines all over my apartment once more. I even started playing cards with my friends again. Randy told me, "I love seeing your zest for life coming back!"

Thinking, reading, talking—even making decisions—got faster and easier. My neurologist tested my brain function and said it had jumped from 77.1 to 95.9!

At my LearningRx graduation, Randy told everyone, "We have our wonderful Virginia back!"

WATCH VIDEO
"Virginia's Story"
Scan with smartphone or visit
vitalconnectionsbook.com

I love being able to do the things I enjoy. Best yet, I know I'm not at the end of my life. I may be eighty-one, but I'm not giving up. I still have a future to look forward to.

—*Virginia Romero*

Life Is a Journey. Take Snacks and a Backpack.

"What if I hate it?"

Ten-year-old Luke waved the question like a bright red flag. His mom, Julie, had just told him he'd be starting brain training at LearningRx; and Luke was dubious about the idea, even though his brother and sister were in the same program and loved it.

His first day at the LearningRx Center in Jacksonville, Florida, Luke frowned as he headed off with his trainer for their first session. Waiting in the reception area, Julie thought about the crazy journey that had led her family to try brain training in the first place.

Two years earlier, Julie's oldest son, Joshua, then eleven, had been diagnosed with ADHD and oppositional defiant disorder (ODD). Searching for answers, Julie visited Internet bulletin boards and consulted doctors. At one point she paid eight hundred dollars for testing that provided labels but no solutions.

Hearing about LearningRx, Julie became curious. Could intense mental exercise really stimulate the brain to strengthen neural pathways, to the point of actually raising a kid's IQ and giving him better skills for school and for life? If so, could it help Joshua? It was worth a try.

Within weeks of starting the program, Joshua was focusing better than ever. Math tests that used to take ninety minutes were now taking twenty minutes or less. And while Joshua's anger and oppositional behavior still flared, Julie realized that LearningRx was removing her son's frustration with learning, thus making it possible for other issues to be isolated and dealt

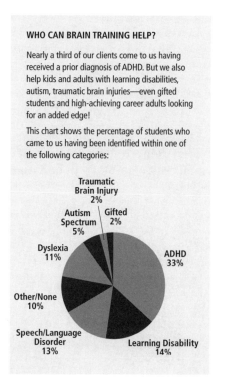

WHO CAN BRAIN TRAINING HELP?

Nearly a third of our clients come to us having received a prior diagnosis of ADHD. But we also help kids and adults with learning disabilities, autism, traumatic brain injuries—even gifted students and high-achieving career adults looking for an added edge!

This chart shows the percentage of students who came to us having been identified within one of the following categories:

Traumatic Brain Injury 2%
Autism Spectrum 5%
Gifted 2%
Dyslexia 11%
ADHD 33%
Other/None 10%
Speech/Language Disorder 13%
Learning Disability 14%

with more effectively.

So when Julie and her husband noticed similar behaviors in their seven-year-old daughter, they didn't hesitate. They enrolled Danielle at LearningRx too.

A week into the program, Danielle sat down and wrote a beautiful story about a family of horses. Julie and her husband marveled that their daughter, who had always believed reading was too difficult for her to master, suddenly had the confidence to tackle writing an entire story!

Before long, Joshua was taking more initiative around the house: washing dishes, vacuuming and organizing. And Danielle performed in a Christmas musical, another surprise. Julie realized that brain training was giving her children confidence and motivation like they'd never had before. Now she wanted the same for Luke, and one day for her youngest son Caden. Julie realized even she and her husband needed brain training!

Julie's thoughts were interrupted as Luke, done with his session, approached her in the reception area wearing a huge grin. "Mom!" he said, "I loved it!"

Pulling into the driveway at home, Luke grabbed his LearningRx backpack filled with brain training games and tools. Julie said, "Baby, leave it in the car so we won't forget it tomorrow."

Luke shook his head. "I wanna keep it with me." That night he slept with the backpack beside him.

LearningRx brain training had been life changing for Joshua and Danielle. What good things were in store for Luke and, eventually, Caden?

Yes, life is an interesting journey. Julie thanked God that she and her husband had found the right partners to help them equip their kids for the trip.

READ BLOG
"Raising 3 Knights
and a Princess"
Scan with smartphone or visit
vitalconnectionsbook.com

Would a Gridiron Concussion Keep David from Landing His Dream Job?

Concussions from school sports were robbing David of his dreams, in more ways than one!

In junior high, David was a wrestler and straight-A student. During one match, an opponent picked David up and dropped him on his head. After that incident David began struggling in school.

His memory seemed to suffer the most. And then the additional head injuries David incurred while playing football in high school only made things worse. Sometimes even in the locker room David couldn't remember the game he'd just played.

Later, in college, David dreamed of being a teacher, but couldn't pass the right exams—even after taking them eight times!

A few years later he graduated from a police academy and began applying for jobs, confident this was something he could do. By then he and his wife, Lorelle, were expecting a baby.

The future had never looked brighter. But repeatedly David's applications were rejected. Why? His test scores weren't high enough.

After applying to fifty-six police departments—without a single job offer—David called LearningRx. He calls what happened next "an awakening" of his brain.

> "I sleep better at night knowing my son has gone through this program. As a cop, David has to think and act fast. He has to make life-or-death decisions. Brain training could save his life one day."
> – Ray, David's father

"Shortly after starting brain training, I remembered a dream I'd had the night before," David says. "That hadn't happened since, well, since I was a kid!

After that, improvements just kept coming." One day while driving on a familiar tree-lined street, David realized that he could see, in his peripheral vision, houses past the trees. For years his field of vision had only included the street and the trees. Brain training was improving his vision! Things were different at home too. Now when Lorelle asked David to get something from the store, he remembered! But the changes

TAKING HEAD INJURIES SERIOUSLY

When the brain is injured, connections between cells are damaged and the processing of information is impacted. The brain training programs developed by LearningRx stimulate the connection systems in the brain. As seen on fMRI scans, our programs, specially adapted for TBI patients, literally rebuild areas of the brain's neural network, enabling TBI and stroke patients to regain lost brain function. The following chart shows the percentile gains experienced by adult clients with TBI after participating in brain training with LearningRx:

PERCENTILE GAINS MADE BY TBI PATIENTS AFTER BRAIN TRAINING

Skill Tested	Percentile Gain
Processing Speed	25
Long-Term Memory	24
Auditory Processing	26
Short-Term Memory	22
Visual Processing	21
Logic & Reasoning	14

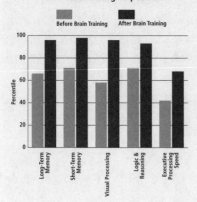

How Brain Training Helped David

went even deeper. One night David asked his wife, "Do you think brain training has made a difference?"

Her answer surprised him. "I feel closer to you," she said. "We have more intimate conversations now. I feel like you really hear me."

David realized it was true. "After brain training," he says, "I could follow my wife better during conversations and remember things we talked about. What a difference that made in our relationship!"

After twelve weeks of brain training, David got a call from a police department that had rejected his application seven months earlier. They said they had another job opening and asked David if he wanted to reapply. That same week, Lorelle gave birth to their daughter, Marlee. It seemed to be the week for new beginnings. This time, David got the job!

David had no idea his dreams were being hindered by those long-ago concussions.

"Brain training changed my quality of life in every area of my life," he says today. "Now I really can dream again."

—*David*

Logan Had Given Up, but His Parents Were Determined to Find an Answer

Guilt. Regret. Questions. These were the things running through Laura's mind as she watched her thirteen-year-old son sulk over the books strewn across the kitchen table. What if she and Ted had kept Logan in preschool longer? What if they had held him back a year in elementary school? Would reading and learning be any easier for him now?

"Logan, you're a smart kid," Laura pleaded. "You can do this. C'mon. Make some sort of effort!"

Every Sunday night through Thursday night, their world revolved around Logan's struggles. From dinnertime till bedtime, Ted worked with Logan on math and science while Laura covered history and English. The couple had three younger children, and Laura wondered how they were being impacted by the hours she and Ted spent every night with Logan on homework, not to mention the stress!

They'd tried a long list of consequences and rewards, but nothing helped Logan tap into a sense of personal accomplishment. Logan was a great kid with a great heart, but when it came to learning, he had given up. Luckily, his parents weren't willing to do the same.

The first thing that attracted Laura and Ted to brain training was how different it was from tutoring. Laura explains, "The last thing Logan needed was to go to Sylvan® and have them do another three hours of what had just been done in school that hadn't worked!"

The second thing they loved was the testing. They'd had Logan tested before, but the LearningRx assessment was the first to explain what was happening in Logan's brain and why he was struggling—and

THE LINK BETWEEN AUDITORY PROCESSING AND READING

Reading, perhaps more than any other academic challenge, depends on strong cognitive skills for consistent success. Efficient auditory processing is at the core of all reading success. Studies by the Department of Education have suggested that poor auditory processing skills contribute to over 88% of the nation's reading problems! On average, after brain training, our clients with moderate to severe cognitive weaknesses experience gains in auditory processing to the tune of 30 percentile points!

+30

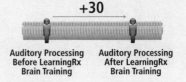

Auditory Processing Before LearningRx Brain Training   Auditory Processing After LearningRx Brain Training

then offer a solution.

"When the LearningRx director here in West Des Moines told us Logan had weak skills in auditory processing, everything started making sense." And because auditory processing is foundational for reading, no wonder Logan hated books!

But the bigger surprise was that Logan actually looked forward to LearningRx brain training. After every session, he couldn't wait to tell his parents everything he had learned and accomplished. His grades improved, and when the opportunity arose to transfer to a more academically challenging private school, Logan was actually excited.

Then there were the books. Discovering a new love for words, Logan read *Treasure Island* with enthusiasm. He talked about the insights he gleaned from what he read. He even asked for books for Christmas. The day Laura walked through the family room and found her son lounging in a chair with his nose buried in a book—for fun—she knew a transformation had truly taken place!

That was three years ago, and Logan is still benefiting from the changes brought about through LearningRx. "When it comes to thinking and learning for the rest of his life, Logan has tools now that he didn't have before," his mother says. "To this day, my husband and I will watch Logan accomplish something new, look at each other and say, 'Brain training made that possible.'"

WATCH VIDEO
"Logan's Story"
Scan with smartphone or visit
vitalconnectionsbook.com

Rescuing a Daughter from Despair

"How long has your daughter been missing?" It was a father's nightmare. Even as I answered the officer's questions, my mind was racing. What else could I do to find her? I'd searched Ariel's school. I'd left messages with her friends. Best I could tell, my sixteen-year-old had disappeared between her last class and getting on the bus to come home.

This crisis was coming after a heartbreaking year or two, with Ariel hanging around with the wrong kids and making some poor choices. The problems began when she started high school. There hadn't been one big sign, just lots of little ones. Like how, on Sunday nights, if my wife or I mentioned school the next day, Ariel's demeanor would change and she'd say "I know" in a defeated voice. Or how I'd tell her about a

book I thought she'd enjoy, and instead of getting excited like she used to, she'd frown and say, "No thanks, I don't like reading." Or the fact that she was spending hours doing homework every night and her grades were still dropping.

I remember looking at one report card and saying, "Honey, you have to get better grades than these." Her voice brimmed with frustration and defeat as she said, "Dad, I can't do it. I'm not smart enough."

A doctor put Ariel on ADD medication, and initially it helped. Then the side effects kicked in: headaches, quick temper, loss of appetite, serious insomnia and depression. She woke up every morning looking drawn and exhausted. Ariel simply gave

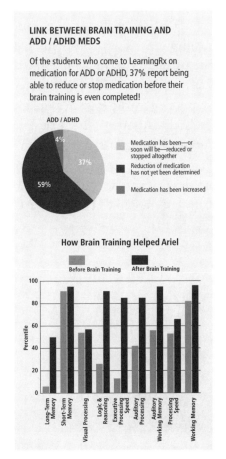

LINK BETWEEN BRAIN TRAINING AND ADD / ADHD MEDS

Of the students who come to LearningRx on medication for ADD or ADHD, 37% report being able to reduce or stop medication before their brain training is even completed!

ADD / ADHD

How Brain Training Helped Ariel

up—on education, on her future, on everything. She started skipping school. Getting in trouble. And now she had run away.

Late that night, we discovered her at a friend's house and brought her home. Ariel was safe—for the moment. But we had to find answers, and fast. We started researching various learning centers and tutoring options. We spent hours talking with people from Sylvan® and other centers. When we saw an ad for LearningRx, we began researching brain training too. I knew we could go to a tutoring center and Ariel would perform better in math or English. But we needed something that would help her with all facets of thinking, learning and life; and LearningRx was the only system that did that.

We signed up for brain training at LearningRx, and just weeks into the program we started seeing changes. Homework took less time and school started making more sense. Ariel also got completely off ADD medications. The brain training exercises got a lot easier too. We did the partner program, where she did half her training at the center and half with me at home. The accomplishments were all hers, but it was something we did together and it was a huge bonding experience for us.

Today Ariel says that LearningRx gave her confidence, hope and a future. She graduated from high school and is going to college. She's going to be a nurse. I watched my child go from having no hope and no thoughts of the future, to having dreams and hopes. I was losing my baby girl, and now I have her back.

—*Danne Zeigler*

WATCH VIDEO
"Ariel's Story"
Scan with smartphone or visit
vitalconnectionsbook.com

Hurricane Irene Forecaster Almost Fired!

"You don't deserve to be in the Navy," announced the lieutenant, speaking for a panel of my superiors. "You're a hindrance. A burden. Dead weight."

I was a meteorologist in the Navy and loved my job. But, honestly, I'd been struggling. Out of every twenty forecasts I'd make, half would have errors; and I often couldn't remember directions or passwords. Still, the lieutenant's next words shocked me.

"You have thirty days to save your career."

It was the ultimate "Shape up or ship out." Scared and upset, I called my family and asked them to pray. I could be fired in a month! I needed help and I needed it fast!

That evening my girlfriend suggested I call LearningRx. Their programs, she said, improved memory and concentration and even raised IQ. With nowhere else to turn, I signed up.

I began meeting with a brain training coach five days a week for twelve weeks. The first week, I still made mistakes at work but was faster at correcting them. Soon I was catching my mistakes before my forecasts left my desk.

A few weeks later, I was driving and looked down to adjust my car's air conditioner. When I looked up, the car in front of me had stopped abruptly—I was speeding at forty-five miles per hour straight toward brake lights! The next thing I knew, I was in the other lane driving smoothly around the stopped vehicle. I was

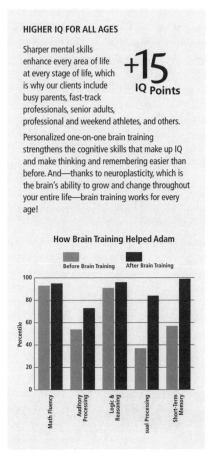

HIGHER IQ FOR ALL AGES

Sharper mental skills enhance every area of life at every stage of life, which is why our clients include busy parents, fast-track professionals, senior adults, professional and weekend athletes, and others.

+15 IQ Points

Personalized one-on-one brain training strengthens the cognitive skills that make up IQ and make thinking and remembering easier than before. And—thanks to neuroplasticity, which is the brain's ability to grow and change throughout your entire life—brain training works for every age!

How Brain Training Helped Adam

Before Brain Training After Brain Training

blown away. I'd never reacted that quickly before. My brain was truly processing information and making decisions faster than ever!

In the following months, I got a promotion. Then another one. Shortly after that, I appeared before a committee to become certified to forecast hurricanes. After an intense round of questioning, they asked me to step outside. When I returned, I looked at everyone's somber expressions and my heart sank. Then I noticed a tiny smile in the corner of the mouth of one officer. He asked, "How do you think you did?"

"I studied hard, Sir. I did the best I could."

He nodded. "You not only passed, Sailor, you gave the best qualification board performance this committee has seen in six months."

The lieutenant who had called me a "burden" eight months before was the first in line to shake my hand.

Recently the East Coast was pummeled by Hurricane Irene. As the storm formed off the Atlantic Coast, the base where I was stationed in Virginia assembled a select team of forecasters to track the hurricane and issue warnings to the military and the public. I was handpicked to join this team.

In eighteen months I went from almost being kicked out of the Navy to being promoted to assistant supervisor and division trainer—and being told I'd become one of the most sought-after hurricane forecasters. God answered my prayers and those of my family. And a big part of that answer was LearningRx.

—*Adam Hill*

WATCH VIDEO
"Adam's Story"
Scan with smartphone or visit
vitalconnectionsbook.com

"Biggest Loser" Stars Get Fit in Body and Brain

Phil Parham dreaded his son's kindergarten graduation. He'd been excited the first time Rhett graduated from kindergarten. He'd even been pleased the second time. But this would be the third time his son, who had been diagnosed with autism, would "graduate" from kindergarten.

As Phil watched all the other parents glow over this milestone in their children's lives, he couldn't help but feel that this "milestone" for his family seemed more like a millstone. Would Rhett ever be able to do well in school? Have a job? Succeed in life?

Phil's wife, Amy, also mourned the loss of dreams for a "normal" life for their son. To cope with the stress and emotional pain, Amy says that she and Phil turned to food for comfort, packing on close to three hundred unwanted pounds between them.

Life changed dramatically for the couple, however, after competing in season six of *The Biggest Loser*. After Phil and Amy lost a combined total of 256 pounds during the hit reality show, they were contacted by Becky McLaughlin, the director of a LearningRx Center near their home.

"I saw your story on TV," Becky told them. "I know your son has autism, and I can help."

The couple was skeptical, having tried every treatment under the sun. But they agreed, and now say that one-on-one brain training has been life changing for their autistic son.

"Doctors had told us there were so many things Rhett could never do," Amy recalls. "Now he's in regular classes, he's reading on grade level, he's doing well in math like never before. We attended LearningRx two years ago, and we're still seeing the results of that training. Rhett is building on the gains that were made during that time. I can't say enough good things about LearningRx."

Phil adds, "Somebody who knew what they were doing came along and helped us dream again and get a new vision for what was possible."

Today the reality-show celebrities are passionate about helping people get healthy, as they travel nationwide conducting "ninety-day fitness challenges." They are also passionate about LearningRx. With a second son currently enrolled in brain training, they're seeing the impact that working with a brain coach can have on entire families.

"Our other son doesn't have autism, but he's a teenager," Phil says with a grin. "Need I say more?"

Phil and Amy have tried brain training themselves, and agree that just as they needed personal trainers Bob and Jillian from *The Biggest Loser* to push them to their best shape physically, working with a personal brain trainer is the most effective way to get in shape mentally.

"People will spend thousands on gym memberships," Amy notes. "But how much more important is it to think clearly? Everybody can benefit from sharpening their brain. There are all kinds of reasons to have a coach for your brain just like you have a coach for your body."

WATCH VIDEO
"Hope for Autism"
Scan with smartphone or visit
vitalconnectionsbook.com

"Your Son Isn't the Same Kid Anymore"

I'll be honest, it hurt to listen to him read. But that wasn't the worst of it. By the time Dillon reached high school, he seemed ticked off most of the time. He was acting out in class. He was disrespectful. Teachers would call me at home and say, "Your son needs to be more respectful in class." As if I didn't know!

At home, I'd tell Dillon to study for a test and he'd refuse. He'd say, "I don't have to study. I understood the homework." And he had. So why did he fail every test?

After we got him tested at LearningRx, it all made sense: Dillon's short-term and working-memory skills were really weak. We came to realize that he really did understand the concepts as he learned them; he just couldn't hang onto them. No wonder he was frustrated and mad at the world.

We had kept thinking Dillon was lazy. To motivate him to work harder, we took his cell phone away, and then we took his car away; but it never seemed to work out like we'd hoped. It makes so much sense, looking back, now that we know what was going on!

Within weeks of starting brain training, Dillon was doing things he never could have done before. The first thing I noticed was that he wasn't spending nearly as much time struggling over homework. In fact, he finished his assignments so quickly that I wondered if he was actually doing the work! The only thing that convinced me was the improvement in his grades, as Cs

READING IMPROVEMENTS

Reading, perhaps more than any other academic challenge, depends on strong cognitive skills for consistent success.

Students who come to us to improve their reading, on average, see a **2.9 year gain in age-equivalent reading skills.**

What's significant is that these gains are consistent regardless of where a student initially ranked in reading. This means that students who test far behind their peers—as well as students who test equal to or even above their peers—still improve their reading skills by about three years.

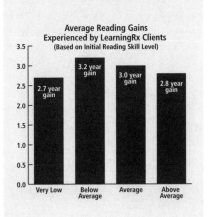

Average Reading Gains Experienced by LearningRx Clients
(Based on Initial Reading Skill Level)

and Ds turned into As and Bs.

Before long, Dillon was using his cell phone at school to snap pictures of As on tests and homework assignments and text them to me, too excited to wait until he got home to show me the good news!

But what I really loved was that Dillon simply became a happier, more confident kid, both at school and at home. Suddenly he didn't have to fight so hard. The kid that teachers used to call and complain about was suddenly behaving better in class. His literature teacher, who had Dillon as a student both before and after brain training, told me my son was a different kid.

Dillon did so well in chemistry that he started tutoring other kids. He actually told me, "Mom, this stuff is easy." I'd never heard that before!

His final year of school, Dillon took the kind of tough classes he never would have attempted before brain training, including honors chemistry and an advanced calculus class.

To this day, Dillon will try something new and say, "Mom, before LearningRx I couldn't have done that."

You can say that again!

—*Shannon Graham*

WATCH VIDEO
"Hope for Struggling Students"
Scan with smartphone or visit
vitalconnectionsbook.com

APPENDIX F:
Answers to the Top Six Questions About Brain Training

You've got questions? We've got answers. From brain training video games to the best age for brain training, here are answers to six of the most common questions about brain training.

Q: What is brain training?
A: Brain training consists of a series of intense mental exercises that strengthen underlying cognitive skills, literally giving kids and adults faster, smarter brains. These underlying cognitive skills make up IQ and equip the brain to efficiently handle day-to-day tasks like thinking, learning, reading and remembering. These cognitive skills can be "beefed up," so to speak. You know how physical exercise gives you a stronger, faster body? Mental exercise—done in the right sequence and under the right conditions—gives you a stronger, faster brain.

Q: Is brain training primarily for children?
A: Not at all. The science of brain training is based on neuroplasticity, which refers to the brain's lifelong ability to grow and change. At every age and stage in life, your brain can increase existing neural pathways and even create new ones. This means the way you think and learn—even your IQ—is never set in stone! It can always be changed and improved.

Q: How do your programs work?
A: Our research-based programs consist of customized mental exercises, done one-on-one with a personal brain trainer over twelve to thirty-two weeks. The "personal training" aspect of what we do is critical, because for brain training to be effective it must incorporate five key elements: practice, intensity, sequencing, loading and immediate feedback. And clearly the best way to accomplish these elements is by working with a personal brain trainer.

Q: Can't I improve my brain by myself, using puzzles and online games?

A: Puzzles and online games are healthy choices. Think of them like eating an apple instead of chips, or taking the stairs instead of the elevator: in other words, a great way to stay healthy and flexible. But for dramatic changes, you need something more! When you're serious about improving your body, you hire a personal trainer. In the same way, when you're serious about improving your brain, you hire a personal brain trainer.

Q: What differences can I expect after brain training?

A: Our students gain an average of fifteen to twenty points in IQ and move up an average of thirty percentile points in mental skills. But we don't just change brains; we change lives. The kids and adults who go through our programs—including those with ADHD, dyslexia, autism and even traumatic brain injuries say the differences in their lives are dramatic! They say they can think, learn and remember better than ever! A faster, stronger brain improves performance at school, at work, in sports—even behind the wheel of a car.

Q: How do I get started?

A: The first step is to locate and call the LearningRx Brain Training Center nearest you. (To find a center, visit learningrx.com). They'll answer any questions you may have, and even give you a free brain training demonstration if you'd like! The next step is to schedule a comprehensive cognitive skills assessment. We use the Woodcock Johnson III, which is the gold standard of cognitive skills testing. You'll learn which cognitive skills are weak, how those weak skills are impacting daily life, and how they can be targeted and strengthened through a customized brain training program.

APPENDIX G:
The Value of a Better Brain: Is Brain Training Worth the Cost?

Brain Training: A Smart Investment

LearningRx brain training, done one-on-one in a coaching environment, raises IQ by an average of fifteen to twenty points. And studies have revealed a direct link between higher IQ scores and higher salaries. In fact, a study by the US Department of Labor Statistics showed that a gain of even ten IQ points can result in a $9,000 to $18,000 increase in annual earnings. Multiply that by forty years of employment and the numbers become even more impressive! LearningRx brain training is proven to increase IQ by an average of fifteen points or more. That means for every dollar spent on brain training, there's a return of $127 over a client's lifetime.

IQ Range	Income at Age 30 (adjusted for 2010)
120+	$83,933
110–119	$71,824
90–109	$62,564
80–89	$46,744
<80	$28,017

How Does Brain Training Compare to Tutoring?

Statistics show that, dollar for dollar, brain training is seven times more effective than tutoring. While the hourly rate for one-on-one brain training is higher than the hourly rate for group tutoring, brain training produces results so quickly that it can cost literally thousands of dollars less than tutoring—and produce the same improvements! Plus, tutoring reteaches information that a student might not have grasped the first time around. Brain training physically reorganizes neural pathways, creating a faster, smarter brain for a lifetime!

Reading Improvements: Average Skills Years Gained

All Small Group Tutoring — 1 Month Net Gains — Tutoring conducted over a school year. Based on results from 30 tutoring companies.

Best Small Group Tutoring — 3 Months Net Gains — Tutoring conducted over a school year. Based on results from the top 6 tutoring companies.

LearningRx Brain Training — 2.9 Years Net Gains — Brain training conducted over 6 months. Based on results from all LearningRx Centers.

Does It Last?

Our programs create results that are dramatic and lasting—and we've got the numbers to prove it! Using the gold standard of cognitive skills testing, the Woodcock Johnson III, we measure the cognitive skills of every client before and after brain training. Whenever possible, we measure again a full year later. But don't take our word for it. Check out these logic and reasoning scores of clients tested before brain training, immediately after brain training, and a year later. Twelve months after completing their programs, our clients retained 103 percent of their gains! That means their improvements have not just held steady but have actually continued to increase!

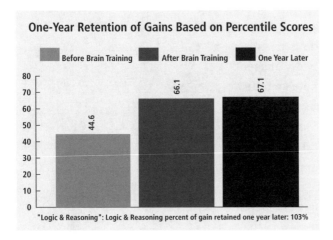

One-Year Retention of Gains Based on Percentile Scores

Before Brain Training   After Brain Training   One Year Later

"Logic & Reasoning": Logic & Reasoning percent of gain retained one year later: 103%

About the authors

Michael J. Klassen has authored five books. He has also ghostwritten or contributed to twenty-two more. When he isn't writing, he enjoys coaching aspiring writers. Michael, his wife, Kelley, and their three daughters live in Littleton, Colorado, where he serves as founding pastor of The Neighborhood Church (www.tnc3.org). To contact Michael or learn more about him, visit www.michaeljklassen.com.

Karen Linamen is the author of sixteen books on strategies for living well, and a frequent speaker and media guest. Her topics include how to improve the quality of your emotions, relationships and dreams, as well as how to use the applied science of neuroplasticity to reap the benefits of a faster, stronger brain. She writes and speaks to women of all ages, as well as individuals and families impacted by learning struggles, ADHD, dyslexia, autism, age-related mental decline and traumatic brain injuries. Learn more about Karen at www.karenlinamen.com.

Tanya Mitchell is Vice President of Research and Development at LearningRx, a national brain training company with more than eighty centers across the country. She has trained more than one thousand psychologists and educational specialists in cognitive skills assessment and brain training methods, and has shared her expertise on radio and television and at conferences around the country. She is also a coauthor, along with Kim Hanson and Dr. Ken Gibson, of the book *Unlock the Einstein Inside: Applying New Brain Science to Wake Up the Smart in Your Child*. To download a free copy of the book, email Tanya at tanya@learningrx.com.

To inquire about media and speaking appearances related to this book:
Email tanya@learningrx.com, visit www.learningrx.com, or
call the LearningRx National Headquarters at 719.264.8808.